CALL BACK
OUR YESTERDAYS

Phyllis Houseman

First printing March 1992

ISBN: 1-878702-82-9

Printed in the United States of America

METEOR PUBLISHING CORPORATION
Bensalem, Pennsylvania

First, to Jack, who keeps me "on line" with his love and unfailing support.

And, of course, to Valerie and Daniel, who have made their mother very proud.

To Margaret Cesa, who generously took the time to share her knowledge of Taos with me.

And finally, to the Peace Corps Volunteers who made up the real Ecuador II. I know there wasn't a green-eyed Mexican-Indian-Irishman in the bunch, but all of you helped make that two-year adventure one of the most important experiences of my life.

PHYLLIS HOUSEMAN

The hero and heroine in the books Phyllis writes tend to fall in love very quickly, just as she did with her husband, Jack—when they were eight years old. Unfortunately, Fate then kept them apart for years. During that time, Phyllis studied biology, was a Peace Corps Volunteer in Ecuador, and taught high school in Detroit, Michigan. But when she finally met Jack again, they got engaged on their third date. After marrying and having a daughter and son, they moved to California where they now live northeast of San Francisco.

Other books by Phyllis Houseman:

No. 65   *TO CATCH A LORELEI*

ONE

Michael O'Brian paced out sunlit squares of kitchen tile, waiting for Jeff to answer the phone. He knew the boy was at home. Since the sixteen-year-old had gotten his license a month ago, Jeff didn't go anywhere on foot if he could drive . . . even the thousand feet that separated the two ranch houses. And through his window, Michael saw Jeff's blue pickup truck parked in the driveway next door.

As Michael listened to the phone ring, that strange prickly sensation he had been feeling all morning long ran down his spine again.

Kachinas dancing on his grave, his mother would call the troublesome itch. The feeling wasn't new, a milder version of it tickled him at the beginning of every laboratory trial of a new drug, or when he had to chair the annual stockholders' meeting. But it hadn't been this strong in years . . . not since Ecuador. Not since the day he had run out on Laura in Quito.

"All right, all right, I'm here!" An exasperated young tenor voice shouted in Michael's ear.

"Jeff! What in the hell took you so long? I was just going to hang up."

7

"Well, Mike, you know about Murphy's Law. If you want the phone to ring, just get in the shower, or go to the toi—"

"OK, OK, I get the picture," Michael chuckled. "Say, Jeff, I wanted to find out exactly when you're going to leave on that fishing trip tomorrow. I know you'll be here to feed the horses for me this afternoon. But just in case something comes up at the conference, and I have to stay overnight in San Francisco, will you be able to take care of them again tomorrow morning?"

"Sure . . . no problem," came the swift reply. "Todd and his folks aren't picking me up until ten or so. You'll be back for sure by tomorrow night, won't you?"

"Of course, even if I'm stuck there this evening, I'll be home before noon."

Michael closed his eyes in disgust at the sound of his glib assurance. He was playing mental games with himself, and he didn't know why. Only forty miles separated his home from San Francisco. After he gave the keynote speech at the American Chemists' Society annual conference, he had absolutely no reason to stay the night at the Sir Francis Drake Hotel.

He really didn't want to take advantage of Kattie's absence to call one of his former acquaintances in the city. He had broken off with them over five months ago, when Jeff's mother agreed to let him "court" her as she put it.

So what if he'd been without a woman in all that time? He respected Kattie's wishes not to rush their relationship. His mind skidded away from the reasons why *he* hadn't pushed to share her bed.

Kattie was on vacation now from her job as a hospital pediatric nurse. She had taken her three youngest children to visit their grandmother in the hills of Arkansas for a couple of weeks. It was the first time Kattie had been back to her birthplace in sixteen years.

Suddenly realizing that Jeff patiently waited on the other

end of the line, Michael tried to get his thoughts back in order.

"Your mom left a message on my answering machine saying that she'd reached Tanner's Creek safely yesterday. Did she also call you?"

"Yeah, and you should have heard her!" The teenager related a pithy description of what his mother had found in the hills and "hollers" of her youth.

"The last outhouse in America, huh?" Michael chuckled. "Well, I know there are a few more around, but won't little Amy have a lot to share during show and tell when she gets back to school in the fall?"

"I'm glad my summer job starts Monday, and I couldn't go with them," Jeff said fervently. "Be my luck to find a snapping turtle in one of those things."

Michael laughed, and then checked his watch. "Well, I've got to go, Jeff. Have a good time on your trip and I'll see you Sunday when you get back. Don't break any fingers."

"Ah, Mike, you're beginning to sound just like Mom. Don't worry, I don't want to arrive at Juillard in September with my hands in a cast. Although maybe that would start a whole new style of piano playing."

Even when he finally cradled the receiver, Michael's smile didn't die. Jeff was a great kid. And he could just hear Kattie speaking in that soft accent of hers, going on about the hillbilly existence she had escaped from sixteen years earlier. Her cheerful, pretty face formed in his mind's eye. She was a delight. Her children—all four of them—were equally wonderful.

No, he wouldn't be staying in San Francisco after the conference tonight. Only a fool would jeopardize what might be his last chance at happiness by giving in to the male hormones coursing through his body.

And fool was not a word that Michael used to describe himself these days. He hadn't merited *that* label in over fifteen years, not since his Peace Corps days and his service in a small South American country.

An unexpected flash of remembrance jolted Michael, as he suddenly saw the tall, skinny kid he had been at twenty-one.

Pushing the image away, he checked his watch again, and then went into the den. Retrieving his briefcase from the top of the desk, he opened it to make sure his speech was inside. Satisfied that all was in order, he grabbed the leather handle and swung the case off the oak surface. Yet, even as he turned to go, his head swiveled back and his eyes drifted to the locked bottom drawer of the desk.

He hadn't opened it in five months. That was another thing he had stopped doing since making up his mind about Kattie. He hadn't read the letters and he hadn't looked at Laura's picture in all that time. He should burn the contents of that drawer, the keepsakes of his Peace Corps service. He had to do it soon.

As he put his briefcase in the trunk of his car and climbed into the Mercedes, Michael had another disturbing recollection of his younger self. This time, the boy he had been was sitting in an airport lounge, waiting for his flight to be called.

Shaking his head, Michael made a vain attempt to stem the vivid memories of that important day. But the mental pictures wouldn't stop. Even as he pulled onto the freeway, and even when he guided the car over the Bay Bridge into San Francisco, he couldn't shut down the ancient film that ran in his mind.

Instead of seeing the striking city skyline, or looking at the Golden Gate Bridge to the north, Michael O'Brian relived the day he left New Mexico for his Peace Corps training. He had been called by a different name then.

"We came to wish you a safe journey to Ecuador, son."

Miguel O'Brian's dark head snapped up from the chemistry book he had been reading. His hybrid eyes narrowed in surprise, focusing on the small delegation his family made in front of him. They were all there—his mother, his three half-sisters, and Will Montoya, his stepfather. They must have started out from the Pueblo de Taos reservation at four in the morning to make it to Albuquerque before his eight o'clock flight left.

Carefully placing the textbook on the leather seat next to him, he slowly got to his feet, once again conscious of towering over everybody when he straightened. Miguel took a step forward and enclosed his mother in the hug she wanted, but never would initiate. After the brief embrace, he held his hand out to his stepfather. Calloused palms firmly reestablished the truce that had been worked out between them only a few years ago.

Miguel looked back and forth between the two high-cheekboned faces. "Mama, Will, I'm really glad to see you. But . . . didn't you get my last letter? I won't be leaving for Ecuador until my Peace Corps training is over, two months from now."

"Of course, we got the letter," his stepfather answered, "or we wouldn't have known that you were flying to Maryland this morning. But it wasn't clear whether or not you would be going straight to South America after your training. So, since the co-op just finished a large order of pottery for the Indian Pueblo Cultural Center here, and I had to come down anyway . . ."

"I'm sorry about the confusion." Miguel broke in before the irritation in Will's voice could degenerate into open hostility. "I thought I had written that I'd be home sometime in late August, no matter if I get through training or not."

But Miguel really didn't believe he would wash out. His skills would be needed too much. How many chemistry majors, fluent in Spanish, could the Peace Corps have recruited to teach in Ecuadorian high schools?

"Anyway, the successful volunteers get a two-week

leave to buy clothing and generally put their affairs in order before they leave the United States,'' he explained.

"Two weeks? And then we won't see you for two years." Elena O'Brian Montoya spoke for the first time. Her tone was flat, unemotional, but the hazel eyes that revealed her own mixed heritage conveyed the censure her voice lacked. Not that her son could blame her for being angry, it had been almost a year since he had been back to Taos.

"*Ka* . . . Mother, I had to work every vacation, and you know the study load I was taking . . .''

"Of course, of course, I understand. That's why I brought the girls with me today, so that you could see them before their weddings.''

A rare smile softened the still beautiful face, as she drew her daughters forward. At three, six, and twelve, it would be a few years before any wedding plans were made, but Miguel's wry grin acknowledged that his mother's gentle barb had hit its target. Looking down on the girls, he realized he barely recognized them.

Paula was no longer a babe in arms. Graciella's shy smile revealed missing front teeth. It was Sara, however, who had changed the most. Her intelligent little face had thinned out. She was inches taller than he remembered— probably near to her adult height. And there were unmistakable signs that she had reached the beginnings of adolescence. But her eyes had altered most of all. Her large, dark irises held none of the exuberant affection she had always bestowed upon her older brother. In its place was a hostile glare and a barely concealed accusation.

The younger girls returned his hugs and kisses, but Sara shook him off.

"*Niña*, what's wrong? Did you have to get up too early this morning? You always were a slugabed.''

Sara would not allow him to tease her out of her anger. "Why are you going to South America?" she challenged. "You were supposed to come home for good after you got your master's degree. You promised us, Miguel, you promised.''

"Sara, don't cry. I know that I said I'd be back this year, but don't you understand that there are a lot of people who need help in Ecuador? I just can't turn my back on them.''

"What about all the people on the reservation? They need help, too. Oh, you just don't want to come back, do you?'' she wailed. "Well, see if I care! See if I write you one measly letter.'' Sara turned to hide her face in her father's shirt.

Over her head, Will nodded. "She's right, you know. There's plenty of good work for you to do at home. We really need somebody with your chemistry background to research the old ways, to find out how they got the colors so bright and how they made them adhere to the pottery so well. Also, I don't have to tell you that Celia has been counting the days for you to get back. Her mother has been very sick, or she would have come along with us this morning to convince you to come home.''

Will was smiling now, but Miguel couldn't match his grin. Celia Ochoa? The girl everyone expected him to marry although he had never proposed to her. Home? The ultra-conservative Pueblo Indian reservation, which banned electricity and running water.

Still, looking at the faces of his only living relatives, Miguel didn't have the heart to tell his family how he really felt. He'd have to reassure them again . . . to lie to them again. Fortunately the announcement calling his flight saved him from adding yet another sin to his tally.

"Good-bye, my son," his mother whispered. "I'll pray that the *Kachinas* weave well for you and bring you safely home.''

When Miguel fastened his seatbelt a few minutes later, he remembered his mother's benediction and shook his head. Even if the ancient Pueblo gods existed, they'd never weave on their celestial loom for him. He had refused to be initiated into the tribe.

Oh, he had wanted to belong; as a child he had yearned to belong, especially after his father had died. But he had been too different. Different beyond his height, different beyond the eyes he had inherited from the Mexican-Irishman, Ramón O'Brian.

No, the reason he had rebelled as he grew older was because he couldn't live by the old ways. He had questioned, he had doubted. He wanted to soar into the future, not be bound by the past. Well, he would have two years to figure out how to break away from that past without hurting his family or Celia.

As the plane lifted off and banked sharply, Miguel looked down at the receding ground. His eyes widened when he suddenly recognized the ancient wood-slatted co-op truck pulling onto the Pan American Freeway. A tiny figure in the flatbed was holding onto the top rail with one hand and waving madly with the other.

Sara—finally relenting—even though she had seen through his excuses about joining the Peace Corps, excuses that he had almost believed himself until this morning.

Oh, he'd be needed in Ecuador all right, and he'd do his very best to represent his country. But twenty-one-year-old Miguel Enrique Vincente O'Brian was well aware that by going to South America, he really would accomplish what he had threatened to do on his eighth birthday. He was running away from home.

TWO

Michael handed over the Mercedes to the parking valet and entered the hotel at a run. He wasn't late for his talk, but he couldn't shake the persistent feeling that something earth shattering would happen if he didn't get to the meeting room quickly.

Maybe they *were* going to have another earthquake. He knew that some people were sensitive to an impending tremor. Although, in the past, he'd experienced more than his share of seismic events, without any physical warning.

Yet, the closer he had gotten to the city, the stronger the tingling along his spine had become. His mother would say the gods were after him.

According to her, the Pueblo deities she worshipped were going to dog him until he came home to make peace with them. And it was true, there had been occasions in the past when Michael almost believed her warnings. The last place in the world, however, he expected spirits to be nipping at his heels was in San Francisco's Sir Francis Drake Hotel.

Michael had to admit that if they actually were out to get him, the gods were really clever this time because they snared him with the lure of infectious laughter.

15

A huge swell of it surged out of a partly closed conference-room door, just when Michael strode down the corridor, determined to get to his 6:00 p.m. meeting. Against his will, he stopped in mid-stride, intrigued by the unrestrained mirth.

Reading a posted sign, he found that the Greater San Francisco Teachers' Association had scheduled a lecture on "The Implementation of Creative Discipline".

Teachers? None he had ever known giggled like that. And even stranger, between the waves of delighted laughter, he heard someone berating the group in a querulous voice. To Michael, it sounded like Hattie McDaniel was giving the spoiled Scarlett O'Hara another one of her Oscar-winning tirades. But what did *Gone With The Wind* have to do with creative discipline, he asked himself.

Michael didn't even think about the crowd of research chemists that would be gathering down the hall for his keynote speech. Forgetting his previous feelings of unease, he rounded the half-closed door and slipped into the packed auditorium.

At the opposite end of the meeting room, a bent figure painfully hobbled toward the back of a bare, dimly lit stage. Outrage radiated from the crippled body, when the poor creature lifted her head as high as a work-twisted spine could manage.

"LeMont, I don't care if it takes us three days to get to your English class!" the old woman grated. "I gots all the time in the world. And even if you is as old as me when you gets done, you is gonna pass the eighth grade. You acted like a clown for the last time, boy. Draggin' your sainted daddy's name down, makin' that sweet teacher cry. Behavin' like you was three years old. Well, a three-year-old is too young to go to school alone. So I'm goin' wit' you, to every class, until you start actin' fourteen, you fool!"

Entranced, Michael watched the one-woman play, as the hobbling actress reached up to grab an imaginary ear on an illusionary six-foot teenager. Michael could almost hear the boy's protests when the woman pretended to drag him to the darkened rear of the stage.

"CUT!" proclaimed a vibrant, husky voice from those shadows. Lights suddenly brightened on the platform, and magically, the twisted old lady gained a half dozen inches, her bowed legs unbent, and her back straightened.

Incredibly, the woman turning to face the audience didn't look anything like the black grandmother Michael had expected. Standing in her place was a slim, golden-skinned blonde, who appeared to be somewhere in her late twenties or early thirties.

As smiling brown eyes scanned the crowd and seemed to lock with his own for an instant, Michael's heart pulsed erratically.

It had happened to him a hundred times before. He'd be attracted to a gleam of ash-blond hair, a glint of honey-colored eyes, or the defiant lift of a rounded chin. Then he'd be compelled to edge closer, to confirm that the woman was *not* Laura. In the last fifteen years, that's just what he had found—a similarity of feature, but never Laura.

He had recently sworn off the habit. He didn't need to search any longer. Kattie was all he wanted now. Yet, even as the thought formed in his mind, Michael narrowed his eyes, forcing them to work to their limit. The hair was slightly darker than he remembered, the figure slimmer. But the eyes were the same, amber brown, with an exotic, catlike tilt to the edges. And her smile—white and even—was the same.

Michael lifted his eyes heavenward, searching for the perfidious gods that had lured him into this room. He wanted to raise his fists in protest, to shout vile curses at those cackling *Kachinas* of his mother's people. There was no mistake—after all this time, when he no longer needed her—they had finally led him to Laura Nordheim.

"Mrs. Mangrum kept her word," Laura was saying into

a microphone near the front of the stage. "She brought LeMont to school every day for the next week, and led him by the hand, or should I say by the ear,"—she laughed—"to each of his classes. By the end of that week, the boy actually went down on his knees, begging the principal and his grandmother to let him go to school alone. He promised to stop his truancy and to buckle down."

Laura surveyed the packed room. The lighting kept her from really seeing beyond the first couple of rows, but using a little trick of the professional speaker once more, she scanned the whole auditorium. Her eyes would seem to touch every person in the hall, creating a greater impact while she summarized her presentation.

"LeMont kept his word, he went to class, did his homework, and eventually graduated, not only from junior high, but from the twelfth grade as well. A miracle? No, only an example of the cardinal rule of creative discipline: You must be consistent. So, I have only one more thing to say before we close this workshop and you go off for your well-deserved vacations. Be consistent, be consistent, be consistent, be . . ." Her voice trailed off, drowned by a tremendous wave of applause.

After the standing ovation, Laura descended from the stage and waited in front of it for the usual questions.

Yes, her inner-city biology classes really had ranked with prep schools in the advanced college placement exams. No, she wasn't teaching in Washington D.C. any longer. She now worked for the consulting firm that developed the techniques that had been so successful with her own students.

As in every presentation she made across the country, the teachers were reluctant to let her go. It seemed that Laura held the key to magic, and they wanted to make sure they really understood the spells she had introduced to them. All of them hoped the incantations would turn them into classroom sorcerers, just like Laura. Finally, the questions flagged and the circle of educators opened up, allowing her to pick up her briefcase and start for the exit.

Nearing the back of the room, she found her eyes drawn to a tall, whipcord-lean man resting against the rear wall. Even after fifteen years, Laura still searched every crowded room and each busy street for similar features. But no one ever matched the face and form that continued to haunt her dreams.

This man was the right height, but he didn't have the painfully thin, young boy's body she remembered. His shoulders were broader, his long legs were more heavily muscled; the fine material of his suit was strained by those full dimensions. Even his face was wrong, it was too hard—all angles and planes—but, without a hint of the vulnerability that should have been there.

Yet, when he pushed himself away from the wall and walked toward her, Laura gasped. It *was* him! Blue-black hair, copper-colored skin, and the glint of exceptional eyes confirmed the man's identity.

The comical thud-thud of two briefcases, hers and his, hitting the floor, neutralized her momentary paralysis.

"O'Brian!" she choked. "It really is you." Without waiting for confirmation, Laura launched herself at him, wrapping her arms around his waist. She hugged him to her, as if afraid he might slip away—as he had done before—as he always did in her dreams.

"Miguel. Oh, Miguel, I never thought I'd see you again," she murmured into the width of his chest.

Strong hands hesitated a painful moment, and then buried themselves in the thick richness of soft, blond hair.

Miguel. Hearing Laura whisper his given name actually hurt. In San Francisco, none of his friends, nobody at the lab, not even Kattie knew that once he had answered to Miguel O'Brian.

Kattie!

Laura felt Miguel tense, and then he abruptly disentangled himself from her embrace. Suddenly, she remembered just how they had parted, so long ago. Her wide smile disappeared, along with the joy she had felt at seeing him again. Taking a step away from Miguel, Laura pulled the mantle of her maturity around herself. She wasn't twenty any longer. The years had proven that friendship lasted longer than infatuation, that love was more trustworthy than passion.

"Well, O'Brian, what have you been doing with yourself?" Laura appraised the expensive cut of his clothes and the wafer-thin gold watch that adorned his wrist. "You're looking very prosperous."

"Things are going well," Michael confirmed, somehow disturbed that the warm glow in Laura's eyes had departed. "I own a small chemical research company in the area." He purposely simplified years of struggle and heartache.

"It's you that's the real surprise, Laura. That skit was fantastic, I never knew you were such a terrific actress! I was just passing by, but your characterization actually pulled me in out of the hallway. You had me and the rest of the audience spellbound." He gestured to the clutch of people still lingering in the center of the room.

Laura turned slightly toward the group. The teachers avidly watched Miguel and herself, perhaps waiting for another emotional display.

Ignoring her burning cheeks, Laura boldly waved to the educators before pivoting back to Miguel.

"Well, my career development is a very long and complicated story, and I'm sure you don't have time to listen to it," she said, glancing at the bulging leather briefcase at his feet.

Abruptly, Laura thrust out her hand. "It really was a surprise seeing you again. Good-bye, Miguel."

Appalled at what her gesture meant, Michael desperately seized Laura's hand and found himself examining the small appendage lost in his. Copper on cream. At one time the contrast had aroused and terrified him.

Now, his old fears seemed ridiculous. The years had given him the confidence he had lacked the last time his dark skin had covered her paleness.

The fear was gone, but suddenly Michael realized the desire was still there. He had absolutely no right to feel such an emotion, yet he wanted Laura as much as he had on that narrow bed they had shared one night in Ecuador.

"Laura, I do have a meeting to get to, but what about later? Let's have a drink."

His voice was darkly husky as he said the words he shouldn't speak. Somewhere, deep in his brain, his conscience told him that he was setting up a situation that might end in disaster. Yet, he still went on.

"Are you staying at the hotel tonight?"

Laura nodded reluctantly. "I won't be leaving for home, for Los Angeles, until Tuesday."

"Then what about getting together at eight-thirty? Let's really catch up, what do you say?"

He could see indecision play across her small, aristocratic features. But finally, as if she also felt the compulsion to continue this unexpected encounter, Laura nodded again.

"That's fine. I'm having a working dinner with some people, but I'll meet you at eight-thirty in the lobby, Miguel."

Two hours later, Laura finished the supper she had barely tasted and said good-bye to the colleagues she had hardly talked to during the meal.

Distracted, bemused, with more than a half-hour to kill, she sat down on a plush lobby chair. Oblivious to the elegant decor surrounding her, Laura let her uncontrolled thoughts spin her back in time, to the day she had first met Miguel O'Brian.

THREE

The University of Maryland campus in College Park was only a few miles from their apartment, but Laura's father insisted on seeing his daughter safely to the school, on his way to the airport in Baltimore.

Laura stood next to Gustav Nordheim while they waited for her father's administrative assistant to get her suitcase.

The limousine's driver took the piece of luggage out of the trunk and transferred it to Jerrold Easten. He, in turn, deposited the suitcase near Laura, on the lowest marble step of the University's administration building.

"I still think you're crazy to do this, Laura." Shaking his sandy head, Jerry's voice vibrated with a rage that surprised her. "But I guess you're a big girl now and don't have to listen to my advice. See you in two years."

The quick embrace and hard kiss on her mouth startled Laura even more than his anger. As Jerrold climbed into the backseat of the limousine, slamming the door shut, she stared at the darkly tinted window for a long second. The young physicist had joined her father's staff when she was ten. In the decade Laura had known Jerrold, he had never raised his voice in anger to her—and he had never kissed her.

She turned back to her father in confusion. "What in the world is wrong with Jerry?"

Her father gave Laura a slight smile. "Perhaps he just figured out what your acceptance for Peace Corps training will mean to him."

"I don't understand."

"No, I can see that you don't," her father agreed, shaking his graying blond head. "Now, you know that the NATO conferences are scheduled for at least ten weeks, so . . ."

A trickle of perspiration ran down Laura's neck as she stood listening to her father's instructions. She lifted away the weight of her thick hair. While a welcomed July breeze played across her skin, she became more and more impatient with the direction her father's farewell lecture was taking.

"Remember, *liebling*, Dr. Kramer is an old friend of mine. If you have any problems, just tell him. He'll get you a line to Paris and . . ."

"Oh, Papa, you promised. You know that I want to do this on my own. You gave me your word it would be different this time."

"*Ja, Ja, madel, nicht zerrenst du.*" Her father didn't seem to realize that he had slipped into German again. In the last year, the language of his youth had been creeping back into his perfect English. "Don't worry so. He won't tell anyone that you're my daughter. I only informed him because it might not be easy to reach me during the conference."

"Gustav, the plane," Jerrold called, leaning out of the car window.

"*Ein bisschen*, just a minute." The older scientist put up a placating hand and then turned back to his daughter. "Now, give me a smile and a kiss good-bye. You don't want to be late for the Peace Corps orientation, and I can't miss that plane."

Laura's annoyance immediately disappeared. It finally

hit her that if she was successful, it probably would be two years before she saw her father again. He would be in Europe during her two-month training period, not coming back to the States until her leave was over and she had left for South America.

They had been separated before, but never for long. And in Ecuador, she truly would be on her own for the first time. Laura wouldn't have her father's name to impress anyone or his influence to ease her path.

Fighting down a wayward urge to go back into the chauffeured limousine with him, Laura gave her father a quick kiss and a desperate hug instead.

"Now, you be careful over there, Papa, and give them hell," she urged.

Picking up her single piece of luggage, she fled up the stairs and pushed through the doors. Laura had charged several steps into the building before she discovered that she was temporarily blinded by the interior gloom. She tried to stop, but her new shoes slid on the polished marble floor and she barreled into someone coming from the other direction.

With her arms windmilling for balance, Laura's suitcase hit something solid. The rebound force yanked the luggage from her hand. She heard it bounce off a nearby wall. The sound was overlayed by a combination groan and curse.

"Have you registered that suitcase as a lethal weapon?" Her victim's voice was deep and the hands that kept her from falling were definitely masculine.

"Oh, my God. Are you hurt? Where did it hit you?"

"Just a bruised kneecap. Don't worry, nothing's broken." A husky chuckle reassured her.

"I'm so sorry. I guess I'd better wait here a few seconds until I can see again. Maryland summer sun is really potent." She directed her apology to the dark shadow that must be his head, about twelve inches above hers.

"This is nothing. You haven't seen sun until you've been to New Mexico," the voice countered.

"Is that where you're from?"

"Ta . . . Ah, I'm from Albuquerque," he confirmed.

"Oh. Well, I live a few miles from here."

"Then, since you're lugging a suitcase around, you must be looking for the Peace Corps orientation."

"That's right, Sherlock Holmes." She laughed. "I'm going to train for the Ecuador II project—science and math teachers."

"So am I. I'll be teaching chemistry."

As her vision finally returned to normal, Laura found that she was looking up into the chiseled face of a lanky young man. She hoped her sudden gasp of surprise really wasn't as loud as it sounded to her ears, but she hadn't been prepared for what she saw.

His face was rugged and pleasantly homely, with bronzed skin stretched tightly over harshly cut bones. His blue-black hair was thick and straight.

But his eyes! He had leaf-green irises, when the rest of his coloring demanded that they should be black. And those emerald-fired lenses seemed to laser right into Laura's soul, stunning her mind and body.

Perhaps he was used to the effect his unexpected irises had on people because instead of telling Laura to close her gaping mouth, he just smiled. It was a wide grin, that tempered the impact of his gaze. The gentle humor in the smile helped Laura regain her composure.

Sticking out her slightly damp hand, she offered, "I'm Laura Nordheim, and I'll be teaching biology. That is, I hope to, if I can learn enough Spanish in the next eight weeks to qualify."

The green-eyed man seemed to hesitate a long second before he took her hand, giving it a short, hard squeeze.

"Miguel O'Brian. If you need any tutoring, I'll be glad to help. I spoke Spanish before I learned English."

He said it almost defiantly, Laura thought. "I'll certainly take you up on that. I have a feeling I'm going to need a lot of help to get through this.''

"Well, let's find Room 107 and see what they've got planned for us," Miguel suggested. Bending slightly, he picked up the smaller, battered suitcase that Laura noticed next to her own for the first time. Retrieving her luggage, she walked with him down the long, dark hall.

Chaos reined in Room 107, with close to a hundred people with their baggage milling around in the medium-sized lecture hall. Laura stood at the doorway, a little disoriented by the confusion. Only when she saw the large signs taped to the walls did she realize that there was some sort of plan to all the commotion.

According to the red-lettered posters, Turkey IV trainees were supposed to form a line against the right wall. Venezuela III people were directed to the back of the room, while Ecuador II volunteers were to meet to Laura's left.

Her group had the shortest line; about fifteen people were in front of her. As she walked forward, she saw that Miguel O'Brian was already in line, three or four people ahead.

Laura tried to ignore the strange feelings that she had been abandoned. *What did you expect him to do, hold your hand through all of this? You're on your own now, and don't forget it,* she counseled herself. Straightening her shoulders, she got behind a red-haired girl.

For all the apparent confusion, Laura thought, the workers seated at the sign-in tables had to be doing an efficient job of sorting out people because the lines moved forward rapidly.

When Laura's turn came, a young man quickly tagged her luggage and tossed it on top of the pile of suitcases already loaded onto a large cart. She watched it disappear out a door just as the man seated behind the table handed her a large manila envelope and an ominously thick sheaf of papers.

"Look these over, and if you don't have any questions, go to your assigned trailer. Your luggage is being taken over to the compound, you can retrieve it over there. It's about a mile away. There's a map of the campus in the envelope, along with today's schedule and biographies of your fellow trainees. You must hand in the finished forms by breakfast tomorrow."

He completed the speech he had obviously been repeating all day and gestured to the pages tacked together with a huge paperclip.

"But . . . but . . ." Laura started to protest, however the man's attention was already centered on the next trainee.

"Look these over, and if you don't have any questions . . ." he droned again.

Laura walked away, shaking her head. More forms! What else could they possibly want to know about her? She had already filled out dozens of pages in triplicate, answering at least a thousand questions. And she had written essay after essay about her goals, her reasons for wanting to join the Peace Corps.

It had taken days to hunt for school records dating back to kindergarten. She had spent a fortune making copies of those files and endless replications of her birth certificate. Then she had to send for college transcripts and call professors and former employers to see if it was all right to use them as references.

Yet, even all her efforts hadn't provided enough information for the government. Wide-eyed neighbors had told her that the FBI, or some such investigative group, had canvassed them, trying to find out if Laura was truly the upright citizen she claimed to be.

And now they wanted her to fill out even more forms! Laura slowly leafed through the pile, rolling her eyes heavenward when she saw that the questions were even more detailed than she had thought possible.

"Excuse me. What do you think this means?" A Texasaccented voice captured Laura's attention. The drawl belonged to a tall, redheaded girl, who stood in front of Laura, pointing to a list set into two columns.

Laura leaned over to look at the sheet more closely. "Oh, that's just a copy of the clothes and things we were supposed to bring along with us. Didn't they send you one?"

"I got a list, all right. But mine mentioned a bathing suit, and look here, this says *swimming* suit."

"Well, that's the same thing, isn't it?"

"Oh no, it's not. Bathing suit means going to the beach and sitting on your towel, putting on lotion and watching out for guys with great buns. Swimming means going into the water and getting wet!"

Laura laughed at the outraged expression on the Texas belle's face. Blue eyes looked indignant for a second, before warming with humor. "I'm Cheryl Ducaine, by the way."

Laura supplied her own name, but she didn't know if Cheryl heard her as the redhead broke in. "Well, I'm not worried, if there's anything to this swimming business, I'll get out of it, somehow. They wouldn't de-select a person just because she's gets hysterical when she sees more water than is needed to fill a bubblebath, would they?"

"De-select?" Laura echoed.

"That's Peace Corps jargon. I have a friend who joined last year and he wrote me all about it. De-select is when they wash you out of the program. Then there's self-selection. That's when you poop out on your own. They're going to force us into all sorts of stressful situations, and . . ."

A rapid fire of Spanish close behind Laura cut into Cheryl's monologue. The redhead finally stopped talking to crane her head past Laura. Her blue eyes opened wide.

"Well, lookie at that," she whispered in Laura's ear. "Isn't he the most unusual guy you've ever seen? You could cut your fingers on those cheekbones, and that hair sure doesn't go with those eyes, does it?''

Laura turned around, but she already knew who had to be standing behind her. Miguel O'Brian was engaged in an earnest dialogue with a petite black girl. Her long red fingernails were jabbing at the papers she was holding, the row of gold bracelets she wore jangled with angry music. Laura's command of high school Spanish wasn't up to understanding more than a word or two of the complaint the striking young woman was making, but she had enough intuition to guess that she must be feeling overwhelmed by the dozen documents she had just been handed.

"She's really black," Cheryl hissed. "I've never seen anyone with skin so black. I wonder where she's from— Puerto Rico, maybe. They're all Americans there, aren't they? Well, I sure hope they don't put her in the same trailer with me." She quickly looked at the papers in her hand. "I'm in number 36, what's your's, Laura?"

Laura leafed through her own collection until she got to room assignments. Somehow she managed not to groan out loud when she looked at the number. "I'm in 36, too," she called over her shoulder, going toward the Spanish-speaking pair to see if she could be of any help.

FOUR

July 14

Dear Papa,

I'm sorry that I haven't written before this, but you can't believe how little free time we have. Today is Sunday, and the training staff has graciously allowed us two hours off this morning to go to church or to catch up on more mundane matters. So, I'll try to fill you in on what's happened during my first week as a Peace Corps trainee.

There were times during the second or third day when I thought it would be my one and *only* week. Then the famous Nordheim stubbornness got into gear, and I decided that they might wash me out, but I would not quit on my own.

This week, things seem marginally easier for me. I think I'll be able to make it through . . . if I just can do the daily mile run fast enough, that is.

Anyway, after I said good-bye to you on Monday morning, I got my room assignment. Actually, it's a trailer assignment, which I share with three other girls. Or should I say, women? No, girls is probably better; we're all fresh out of college, and as usual, I'm the youngest in the bunch.

The trailer is about thirty-feet long, divided into two living sections, with a bathroom in the middle. Each section has a bunk bed, a double wardrobe closet, and two desks. I share my side with a girl named Kathy. She's from Wisconsin and is one of those beautiful over-achievers that you love to hate—but can't—because she's also one of the nicest, most helpful human beings you'll ever meet. Kathy is a math major, with a minor in Spanish. She lived a few years in Mexico, so she's absolutely fluent. She also earned a letter in track in high school, and leaves me in her dust during our daily mile run.

Then again, *everyone* leaves me in their dust on the track, even Mary Brown, the oldest female trainee at fifty-four. If I wash out, I'm afraid it's going to be for not being able to run the mile in under ten minutes, which they say a healthy twenty-year-old like myself should be able to do easily.

Well, to get back to my trailer-mates—on the other side. Marilynn is from California, and I really don't know too much about her yet . . . she's very quiet and you tend to forget she's there.

Her roommate, Cheryl, certainly makes up for Marilynn. Cheryl never shuts up. She has this whiny drawl, opinions on everything and everybody, most of them sarcastic, or malicious, or bigoted. Even though she grew up in El Paso, she doesn't know a word of Spanish. But she sure knows every racial putdown, which she liberally applies to just about everyone in our melting-pot group. Yesterday, I had enough of Cheryl's verbal poison and I gave her the lowdown about my own ethnic heritage. She's been avoiding me ever since. Terrific!

I don't know how she got through the screening process, and I predict an early de-selection for her. "De-selection" means that they ask you to leave the training program. It's funny, even though we've only been here a week, I bet I can predict who's going to make it, and who won't. Also, who is going to be a "Super Volunteer".

It seems that each group that goes overseas has a couple of Volunteers who, by the force of their personality, will make a lasting contribution to the community in which they serve. We had one of these types speak to us last night at a rally-like session, complete with inspirational slides showing the village he had worked in.

I'll bet Kathy becomes one of the superstars, along with another trainee, Miguel O'Brian . . . that's right, *Miguel* O'Brian. Talk about the American melting pot! Anyway, it says in his biography write-up that even though Miguel has just turned twenty-one, he already has his master's degree in chemistry. He also was an all-conference medal-winner in track. He's another one of those people who always has time to lend a helping hand. Maybe I should get him to give me a few pointers on running before they wash me out entirely.

Well, speaking of washing, I've got to get a load of clothes done, and then it's off to another seminar on Ecuadorian culture. Say hello to Jerry for me, and please explain why I haven't written him. Let him read this letter if he wants.

I've been keeping track of your progress, and I'm glad to see that the arms limitation clause is still part of the treaty. Hope nobody chickens out at the last minute.

All my love,
Your foot-sore daughter, Laura.

August 1

Dear Marthe,

Hope you are enjoying your vacation with your family in Munich. I'm writing you in English because my instructors say that I have to put German out of my mind right now, or I'll never learn enough Spanish to communicate in Ecuador. As it is, my Spanish definitely has a German accent.

Anyway, dear, I haven't forgotten you, or the wonderful care you've given me and Papa over the years. What I wouldn't give for some of your strudel right now. Although perhaps it's best that you're thousands of miles away, and there's only college cafeteria food to tempt me here because I'm on a diet. I've tried every other way to run faster, and hopefully, a little less of me will finally get around the mile track in under ten minutes.

But just wait until September 15th, when I come home for my two-week leave before going to Ecuador. Marthe, you better lay in a good supply of that strudel, and sauerbraten, and kuchen. Ach, it will be heaven!

Love, Laura.

"Well, losing ten pounds hasn't helped one bit," Laura groaned, feeling her muscles cramp up and stumbling to a gasping stop, with more than a quarter mile still to go.

If a strong hand hadn't caught hold of her arm just then, she would have tumbled to the hard-packed cinder track.

"Bend over, Nordheim. Keep your head down, breathe in through your nose and out of your mouth."

It's disgusting, Laura thought in the midst of her agony, *Miguel O'Brian has lapped me three times and he isn't even winded!*

"Oh, leave me be, Miguel," she managed to gasp. "I

just want to die here in peace. It's hopeless, I'm a klutz. I'll never make it through the halfway selection board tomorrow. They're going to wash me out. No matter how hard I try, I'm never going to be able to get my time down to under ten minutes."

"You're not a klutz, and even if you were, it's not a terminal condition. Besides, they're not going to wash out anybody who's trying like you are, Laura. But I know you can break that ten-minute barrier. You're just not running efficiently. I've been watching you and trying to figure out the problem."

Laura's head snapped up, a jolting thrill of pleasure shot through her. Miguel O'Brian had been watching her? It didn't seem possible that she hadn't noticed because she had been watching *him*, ever since that first day of training a month ago.

She hoped he didn't realize how often her gaze turned toward his tall, lean form. Or that his very presence made it difficult for her to keep her mind on her studies. It didn't help her concentration that they were thrown together constantly, in class, in study groups, and even while walking between buildings.

Although Miguel was always friendly, Laura never knew until now that those marvelous green eyes had ever singled her out for special notice. Bemused, she found herself following the first few instructions Miguel threw at her.

"Come on, Laura, shake out your arms. Good. Now, pull each knee to your chest. OK, why don't you run a few steps for me."

Run! She didn't even have enough breath left to voice the word.

"Hey, I never thought you'd be a quitter, Nordheim," he goaded when she tried to wave him away.

A quitter? Well, he had finally found the right key; Nordheims didn't quit! Jarred into motion, Laura managed a staggering step, and then another and another.

"OK, that's enough," Miguel relented. "I think I finally know what you're doing wrong. Who ever told you to run on the balls of your feet?"

Laura shrugged. "I've always run that way. It seems . . . I don't know, more feminine . . ."

"Feminine!" He chuckled. "Well, maybe it works when all you have to do is catch a taxi, but not on the track. For serious running, you should put your heel down first and then push off with your toes. Try it. Down on the outer part of your heel and then push diagonally toward your big toe. Come on, Laura, give it a try. Heel–toe, heel–toe, heel–toe."

She did her best to follow his instructions, while Miguel paced her to the finish line. Then he insisted that Laura try another lap on her own.

"Another lap? Do you want me to die?" she protested.

He didn't say another word, but those narrowed eyes looked slightly disappointed. That was enough impetus for Laura to put one foot in front of the other again, her mind chanting heel–toe, heel–toe. Incredibly, after the first few yards, she found a rhythm in her running that she had never achieved before.

Instead of moving like the Little Mermaid, who took each step in agony, Laura suddenly felt light and bouncy on her feet. And with the pain gone, her lung power proved more than adequate to supply her oxygen needs over the mile course.

"Eleven-fifteen," the coach called out when she ran across the line. "You've taken two minutes off your best time, Nordheim . . . way to go." The fitness expert, who had been taunting her for the last four weeks, actually smiled!

Why hadn't *he* noticed that she had been running the wrong way all this time? *Some expert*, Laura scoffed to herself.

"You just better have that watch ready tomorrow, Mr. Lewis. Wait until I'm fresh," she challenged, throwing

Miguel a grateful smile and taking off at a trot for the women's shower room.

The very next morning Laura broke the awful running barrier with seconds to spare. Miguel tossed her a salute and a smile as an extra reward. Actually, his approval came to mean more to her than anything else, and Laura worked like crazy just to have that grin directed at her again.

It might have been her imagination, but it seemed that after she conquered the track, Miguel actually tried to find excuses to be with her even more than before.

Oh, he always had a good reason. He helped Laura with Spanish vocabulary and gave her hints to improve her accent while they walked between classes. He quizzed her in the library on organic chemistry formulas and lab preparations. And during the weekly lineup in the infirmary—when they received the multiple injections they needed to stay healthy in Ecuador—Miguel surreptitiously gave Laura a firm hand to hold, as the needle slid into her other arm.

Although she treasured their time together, as the weeks passed, Laura became more and more frustrated. He was always there for her, but she also wanted to be of some assistance to Miguel, and there didn't seem to be any way for her to help him.

Besides being revoltingly physically fit, he was also brilliant. An expert in his own field of chemistry, Miguel was terrific at higher math, and he knew more about biology than Laura did. So far, the only thing she had been able to do for him, was to lend him her travel iron when the one provided in the laundry room broke down.

The situation continued until the last week of training, when Laura finally found a flaw in Miguel's perfection.

One morning, instead of their usual exercising, their instructors brought out a phonograph, insisting that old-fashioned social dancing was a grace that would be required of them in Ecuador. There was a lot of moaning and groaning among the volunteers when they were told to pair off.

Looking around for someone to dance with, Laura noticed Miguel inching away from the cluster of trainees. Moving with none of his normal agility, he actually stumbled over his feet. Seeing that Miguel's face was pasty under his copper skin, she suddenly realized that this young man wasn't just peeved at the idea of dancing, he was absolutely petrified!

Grinning widely, Laura moved to intercept him, as he aimed for the back door of the gymnasium and freedom. Coming up behind him, she grabbed the deeply tanned hand that was just about to push the door open.

"Gotcha," she crowed, smiling up into his startled green eyes. Laura placed his hand on her waist and stretched an arm way up to encircle his shoulder.

"Oh, hi, Laura. I just remembered that I've got to finish that research project for Ecuadorian Studies," Miguel said, trying to pull away.

"Oh, no you don't," Laura protested, holding on tight. "You're not going anywhere. Not when I've finally found something I can teach you."

"Ah, Laura, have some pity. I don't know the first thing about this. I'll make a fool of myself."

"Just like I did yesterday, when I 'drowned' in the pool during survival swimming lessons? Or the day before that when I couldn't climb the ladder to get over the obstacle course wall? Come on, O'Brian, let me show you how to dance. You wouldn't want them to wash you out for such a dumb reason, would you?" she asked sweetly.

After staring down at her for ten long seconds, Miguel finally grinned. "OK, you win, Nordheim. Some brilliant guy once said that being a klutz isn't a terminal condition."

As the record started, Laura demonstrated a simple two-step. Miguel spent the first few minutes in utter concentration, watching his feet and counting under his breath. But within a quarter of an hour, he had mastered the basics; and near the end of the session, he subtly took over the lead, turning Laura in perfect time to the soft, slow music.

With the need to monitor Miguel's feet gone, Laura found her senses responding to him on a totally different level. He smelled so clean, so male. Without thinking about it, Laura turned her nose into the thin T-shirt material stretched across his chest. She wanted to incorporate his special essence into her memory.

Feeling a wave of some unnamed longing wash over her, Laura's rhythm faltered. She stumbled on Miguel's toes, and then had to wrap her arms tightly around his slim waist to keep from falling. Miguel swayed against her, pulling Laura closer, until their bodies touched everywhere. Laura thought he muttered something into her hair, and in the same instant, she felt him tremble. A hard, throbbing pulsation grooved into the soft muscles of her stomach where the contact between them was most intense.

Laura's head snapped up, she devoured Miguel's face with hungry eyes. How could she ever have thought that he was homely? He was absolutely gorgeous! And . . . and, she was desperately in love with him. A swift, hot flush of confusion swept across her cheeks when those twin realizations hit her. She looked helplessly into the narrowed green gaze that scanned her features.

Fearing that everything she was thinking was nakedly exposed to his examination, Laura uttered the first words that came into her head.

"Sorry, once a klutz, always a klutz," she said, referring to her mashing of his toes.

The hot light in Miguel's eyes seemed to flicker and die. He cleared his throat. "No, no . . . I'm the one who's sorry," he rasped.

The dancing lesson ended on that ambiguous note. Miguel released her from his embrace, and from that morning until the end of their training, five days later, he avoided Laura.

She saw him only from a distance. He would be walking out of the cafeteria when she came in. During classes, he sat at the other end of the lecture hall. And on the track, he ran well ahead of her—completely out of reach.

Final choices were made at the end of the week. Of course, Miguel and Kathy made it . . . and so did Laura. She couldn't believe it when she found out that Cheryl, the loudmouthed bigot, also would be going to Ecuador as a full-fledged Volunteer.

Laura was torn between her elation and her sadness when she found out that two of the original eighteen had been de-selected. Marilynn, one of Laura's trailer-mates, didn't make the cut. In spite of everything Laura and the others had tried, Marilynn never got over her shyness enough to become part of the group.

The other person to be de-selected was a sweet and funny older man, a retired college geology teacher, who was an expert in Cretaceous fossils. The grapevine hinted that he had tried to hide a serious muscular degeneration problem.

After brief leaves at home, all the Volunteers converged on Miami's airport, late one September evening. Their Pan Am flight lifted off near midnight and left behind the lights of the Florida Keys soon after. An hour later, they passed over sleeping Jamaica, the last bit of land they would cross until morning.

Laura thought she would be too excited to sleep, but by three in the morning her animated conversation with her seat-mates sputtered and finally died. Five minutes later, her head nodded toward the window frame and she was asleep.

It might have been part of her dream, but sometime toward morning, Laura stirred, feeling eyes carressing her slumber-flushed face and tousled hair. Through half-raised lashes, Laura thought she saw Miguel standing in the dimly lit aisle, looking down on her. She wanted to reach out, to smooth away the harsh lines that shouldn't be etching his young face. But she was so tired, so weary. All she could do was slip back into the sensual dream she had been having and fiercely clutch her pillow closer to her breast.

Breakfast was served just before they touched down in Panama. After a quick refueling, the plane lifted off for their final destination, Quito, the colonial capital of Ecuador.

The nebulous geography lessons of the last months became solid reality when the aircraft circled the volcano-rimmed city. Gazing at the avenue of perfect cones, their names echoed poetically in Laura's mind: Cotopaxi, Gentle Neck of the Moon; Tungurahua, The Altar; El Corazón, The Heart.

When the plane found a friendly thermal to cushion its descent, Laura looked down on the closest volcano . . . Pichincha. It was eroded—tamed—and cut into a patchwork design by frugal Ecuadorian farmers. Below that gentled mountain, the ancient city of Quito nestled into the rich lava soil the volcano had spewed out during the wild days of its youth.

Upon landing, they went to the three-storied house the Peace Corps had rented for office space. After being assigned rooms in nearby pensiones, the group's two-week acclimation began.

Miguel's strange behavior continued during those confusing, tiring days. Oh, he was friendly enough on the surface, laughing and joking about their problems adapting to the ten-thousand-foot altitude and the strange new food, but Laura never saw him alone. There were always others included in any meal they shared or conversation they had.

After the orientation, they were all given teaching assignments. Laura could hardly hide her laughter when she heard that Cheryl Ducaine had been teamed with Carmen

Rodriguez. The Puerto Rican biologist was the same dark-skinned girl Cheryl had been so afraid to share a room with on that first day of training.

Carmen barely spoke English, and Laura knew that Cheryl had only scraped through her final Spanish test by the skin of her teeth. Although she felt sorry for Carmen, Laura thought the assignment was a delicious inspiration of some wickedly vengeful god.

When Laura learned of her own placement, she wondered which of the pantheon of deities *she* had offended. To her dismay, she was posted in San Gabriel, a tiny village near the northern Columbian border; while Miguel O'Brian went south to Loja, a city close to Peru, more than three hundred miles away.

As the months went by, some of the aching hurt she felt at their geographical and emotional separation lessened. Her work was demanding, her students were eager and quickly became precious to Laura. The family she boarded with included her in their social life and took her on weekend excursions to the small *finca*, or farm, they owned on the crest of the Andes.

Laura enmeshed herself into the daily fabric of life in San Gabriel. Within four months, she was dreaming in Spanish. Even eating meals in the kitchen where guinea pigs lived didn't seem strange anymore. It was only when the friendly little fluff-balls turned up as the entrée of a holiday meal that Laura knew she wasn't quite a native yet. But she somehow managed to get through her serving by telling herself she was eating chicken.

After eighteen months in the country, although still mindful of the need to supervise the preparation of her food, Laura finally gave up trying to explain her dietary needs to the tiny Indian cook, who spoke more *Quechua*, the language of the Incas, than Spanish. Her capitulation turned out to be a very bad mistake.

A nagging little pain developed in Laura's right side. The ache didn't worsen, but when she went into Quito for

a bi-monthly meeting it was still there, and she mentioned
it to the Peace Corps doctor. Using the resources of a
local hospital run by Canadian medical missionaries, he
ordered several tests. The blood-work report came back
within a half hour. It showed that Laura had an elevated
white cell count. Two days later, the number was high
enough for the doctor to suspect an inflamed appendix and
suggest exploratory surgery.

Laura didn't want to be caught in primitive San Gabriel
with a hot appendix, so she consented to the operation.

When it was removed, the doctors found that her appendix was tiny and pink, and absolutely normal! Later that
day, a report on other tests the Peace Corps physician had
ordered finally made its way out of the overworked lab. It
seemed that Laura really had an intestinal parasite, Giardia
lamblia. The organism could have been eliminated with a
very effective medication; medicine the doctor immediately prescribed for her.

Still in a haze of pain, Laura took the news with the
calm fatalism she had developed in her months of dealing
with the "*Ya, mismo*" philosophy of South America.

Ya, mismo. Sure, I'll be happy to do that for you, right
away . . . soon . . . maybe.

On the second day after her surgery, Laura's discomfort
had diminished enough so that she began to take an interest in her surroundings. She listened to her nurses buzz
about another gringo.

It seemed that the unfortunate fellow had just been admitted to the hospital, the victim of a dog bite—a rabid
dog bite. His wound had been stitched up, and he was
undergoing the very painful series of anti-rabies shots.

After another day of hearing how *macho* and *simpático*
and *guapo* this person was, Laura decided to see the brave,
charismatic, handsome paragon for herself.

Holding her hand firmly over her incision, she rolled
off the bed. Struggling into her robe, Laura made her

way down the corridor with a slightly bent over, shuffling walk.

Her countryman's door was wide open. Straightening as much as she could, Laura took a deep breath and walked into the dimly lit room.

"Hi, there, I'm Laura Nordheim. Haven't you heard that it's more newsworthy if man bites dog? Oh, n–no!" Her voice faltered to a stuttering finish when she got a good look at the rangy figure stretched out on the narrow hospital bed. "N–no, not you, Miguel!"

FIVE

Miguel jackknifed into a sitting position, his green eyes burning in an unnaturally pale face.

"Laura? His gaze searched her robed body. "*Por Dios*, Laura, don't tell me that you're the appendix!"

She didn't want to laugh, but it was useless. Doubling over, Laura tried to keep her stitches intact, as she gave in to a fit of giggles.

Instantly, Miguel was next to her, guiding her to his bedside chair. "Laura, calm down. Please stop, you're going to hurt yourself, *querida*."

At the sound of the unexpected endearment, Laura's laughter abruptly halted. She looked into Miguel's eyes, trying to penetrate their drowning-green depths, to see into the mind that dwelt within.

All she could make out, however, was concern and pain. Her gaze swept over the tightly stretched skin of his face, passing down to his body. For the first time, Laura noticed the wide white bandage on his thigh, peeking out from beneath the too-short hospital gown.

Not even realizing what she was doing, Laura reached out trembling fingers to touch the edge of the dressing. Inadvertently, she grazed the firm warmth of his bare skin

45

and instantly jerked her hand away. She had to fight to keep from rubbing her fingers. They tingled like she had jammed them into a high voltage electric socket. Laura desperately tried to cover her confusion with a rush of words.

"That's where it bit you. My God, Miguel, a rabid dog! How did it happen? What do the doctors say about your chances . . ."

Laura bit her tongue. *Stupid, stupid, stupid,* she silently berated herself. Maybe Miguel hadn't been told about the statistics. Tears welled up in her eyes, realizing how unthinkingly cruel her question was.

Instead of being angry, Miguel put a comforting arm around her shoulders. "Don't cry, Laura. You didn't let the cat out of the bag. I know that the serum only works *most* of the time. All I can do is wait, and I'm damned scared."

A look of surprise crossed his face, as if that admission had not been what he planned to say.

Her heart aching for him, Larua bent forward, cupping her hands on the hard bones of his cheeks. "Please let me wait with you, Miguel. It won't be so bad if we're afraid together."

Miguel's long fingers covered hers. Laura tried to suppress the thrill of desire that raced through her body at the feel of his rough-skinned fingers gently touching her own hands. It was ridiculous to need Miguel like this when her body hurt so much, when he was so injured.

Yet, when Miguel carefully pulled her into his arms, Laura wanted nothing more than to sink with him onto the nearby bed and show him just how much she loved him.

The nurse who entered the room a minute later ended that particular train of thought. But not before Miguel had hugged Laura against his chest and murmured a Spanish phrase into her ear.

Laura heard him whisper, "*Juntos, querida, siempre, juntos.*" Together, darling . . . forever.

*   *   *

They were released from the hospital on the same day. Not being fit enough to return to the relatively primitive towns where they worked, they were temporarily housed in a small pensione near the Peace Corps headquarters. Their rooms were right across from each other and they shared the same tiny table during meals.

Still a little unsure of the nature of the commitment he had made to her in the hospital, Laura waited for Miguel to say something, do something—anything—to clarify his feelings for her.

To her growing dismay, he seemed to have forgotten his binding words. Oh, he didn't avoid her, as he had done during the last days of their training. He couldn't! Not only did they eat together, but after Laura's stitches were removed and the doctors confirmed the success of Miguel's treatment, they also worked together at Peace Corps headquarters.

Each day became a sweet agony for Laura. She was so close to Miguel, and yet, he was so distant. In the evenings, they went on long strolls. But all they shared was the thin, pine-and-dust scented air of Quito.

Miguel didn't touch her, not even to hold her hand. And never once did he refer to those moments in the hospital. Laura found herself searching his face all the time. But she saw nothing in Miguel O'Brian's gorgeous green eyes to indicate that he felt anything deeper than casual friendship for her.

Then one Friday evening, a few days before she was scheduled to return to San Gabriel, they sat down to eat dinner and everything changed between them.

When they finished dessert, Miguel indicated a folded newspaper next to his place setting. "What do you say about taking in a movie, Laura?"

She nodded her agreement, and he turned to the entertainment page. "Hey, believe it or not, *2001* is playing at the Simón Bólivar. I'd sure like to see it again, how about you?''

"I'd love to, and maybe this time I'll even understand it!'' she said lightly, trying to match his mood.

"Yeah, I know just what you mean,'' Miguel chuckled as they went to get their jackets.

They watched the long, strange film in complete silence. The walk back to the pensione, however, was anything but quiet. They dissected the movie, scene by scene, idea by idea, effect by effect.

Climbing to the second floor of the pensione, they were still going at it very loudly when they got to Laura's door.

Inserting her key and giving the lock a twist, Laura vehemently shook her head.

"I'm telling you, that baby did have Dave's eyes. Those monoliths must have rejuvenated him and changed him into some sort of all-powerful being,'' Laura insisted.

"Yeah, sure, 'Superfetus,' '' Miguel scoffed.

While his exasperated voice echoed down the hall, muffled grumblings and rude, sleepy curses floated out from several doors. Startled, Laura and Miguel looked at each other. That was a mistake. A geyser of unrestrained laughter erupted out of them.

It was the final straw for one disgruntled guest, who flung open his door and appeared in the hall, looking angry and very silly in his red-striped nightshirt.

"*Gringos, locos*. Go home, to let me sleep in pieces!''

Knowing that disaster was seconds away, Laura impulsively grabbed Miguel's arm and yanked him into her room.

Slamming the door, she tried to stifle the giggles that were bubbling up her throat. But it was no use. In desperation, she threw her arms around Miguel's waist, and buried her face in the warm expanse of his chest.

His own laughter was muffled in her hair. His arms tightened around her body, trying to steady them as their convulsive mirth threatened their balance.

Laura never knew just when humor fled and something else took over. All she could ever remember was that at some point, she looked up into the green moonlit glint of Miguel's eyes. She was just in time to see them close tightly and hear him groan.

"I need you so much, Laura, and I can't fight it any more!" With the anguished admission, Miguel's mouth found hers.

Nothing had prepared her for the hunger of that kiss . . . his and hers. It seemed like they had been fasting all their lives in preparation for this feast. Her lips instantly opened to the force of his searching tongue. Hers answered his quest with a heat that drew a deep moan from him. As one, they moved a step toward the narrow bed that hugged the near wall of the tiny room.

Strong, gentle hands explored; lean, dark fingers learned secrets that Laura had never revealed to anyone else. It was only when the last barriers of clothing vanished from between their bodies, and hard masculine sinew strained toward yielding feminine flesh, that the reality of what they were doing—the danger of it—exploded in Laura's brain.

"Oh, Miguel, we can't! Your poor leg, my incision, we can't," she wailed.

Poised over her, Miguel's face suddenly reflected all the discomfort that the heat of passion had masked.

"God, Laura, I'm sorry. I wasn't thinking, I was just feeling," he choked, running a healing hand next to the still-raw line that marred the perfection of her skin. Clumsily twisting his body away from hers, he sat on the edge of the bed and reached out shaking fingers for the clothing scattered on the floor.

Before he could put on anything, Laura grabbed his shoulder. "Miguel. Please, dearest, don't go. Hold me, and let me t–touch . . ." Her tongue may have stuttered, but her hand obeyed her heart, boldly caressing down his body, only to hesitate on the tense muscles of his uninjured thigh.

"Laura . . . don't . . . don't stop."

Miguel took a deep, shuddering breath when Laura's fingers moved again—softly, slowly—inching up his leg, until she finally touched the hard length of him.

"Yes! Oh God, yes, Laura."

Abruptly dropping his shirt, Miguel turned into her caress, moving to lie next to her once more. He guided his own hand to her warmth, his fingers twinned her stroking movements.

Hands cupped, fingers played, mouths clung, until pleasure shuddered from one to the other. Their bodies may have remained separate, but Laura felt that their emotional beings had been united by the sensations that shimmered between them.

Even afterward, she found that she couldn't keep her hands off Miguel. In the moonlight that revealed her lover, she traced along the width of his shoulders, up the strong column of his neck, and across the uncompromising line of his jaw.

"You're so beautiful!" The heartfelt compliment was more a sigh then a sentence.

For a minute Miguel just stared at her, and then a deep chuckle rumbled in his chest.

"I think that's supposed to be my line, sweetheart." He grinned, touching her pale skin with his dark hand. "I also think you were very lucky to have gotten through two months of training, without the Peace Corps realizing that you're legally blind."

"Hah! If I'm blind, I'm not the only one," Laura retorted.

"What does that mean?"

"I mean that a few days before we left Maryland, the female trainees in our group got together for an overage pajama party." She smiled, remembering that all-night session. "Someone snuck in some awful red wine that we managed to down. Then, at about two in the morning, we got to discussing men in general—and all you guys in particular. Everyone agreed that Tom Silber was the best looking. But then we voted on which one of you we'd most like to find in our beds."

Laura laughed out loud at the look she saw on Miguel's face.

"Now, don't tell me you fellows didn't have similar sessions," she challenged.

"Well, yes, of course. That's normal, for men," he protested.

"Chauvinist! You don't think I'm going to tell you the rest of this after that remark, do you?" She huffily turned her back on Miguel, but spooned her body into the curve of his, not wanting to lose contact with him even in the midst of her mock outrage.

Stroking the smooth line of her spine, Miguel gently bit her earlobe and coaxed, "Laura, I didn't mean to insult all you lovely women. Come on, honey, tell me. After surviving a rabid dog, you wouldn't want me to die of curiosity, would you?"

She couldn't resist letting her silence lengthen a dramatic second longer.

"Laura!"

Laughing, she turned to face him and ran a teasing fingernail over the hard, flat planes of Miguel's chest and stomach. He sucked in a ragged breath and was reaching out for her when she wickedly announced, "It was seven to one in your favor."

At first he just looked confused, and then totally stunned. "Well, I'll be damned," he finally muttered, "Seven to one? Who got the other vote, Tom?"

"No, Jim Pfeiffer."

"Jim! Why, he's losing his hair and has teeth like Bucky Beaver."

"Yeah, but love is blind. Carol voted for him, and you heard that they got married six months ago, didn't you?"

"Married?" Miguel murmured. "Yeah, married." His index finger began tracing a line down Laura's cheek. "Well, Laura Nordheim, since I'm in such demand I guess you'll want to marry me—before any of those other ladies can track me down."

"Marry? You . . . me? Oh, my God!" Laura fell back in a dazed silence, not seeing the expectant smile on Miguel's face falter and then disappear.

It was only when she felt his fingers dig convulsively into her arms that Laura realized Miguel was still waiting for some sort of answer.

"Of course, I'll marry you! I've loved you since, since that wonderful dancing lesson. But, how . . . when did you . . ."

"Oh, much longer than that. When you were dragging yourself around the track, I guess. Yet, even in my most erotic fantasy, I never imagined that I had a chance with you. And believe me, I dreamed of you every night, and woke up hard and hurting every morning."

"Miguel, you've got to be kidding," she said, glad he couldn't see her blushing. "Didn't you notice me staring at you all the time? I went around with my tongue hanging out whenever you came near me. You must have known how I felt."

"No, no I didn't. Oh, I knew that you *liked* me. But, remember that infamous dance?"

"How could I ever forget it?" Laura teased.

"No, I mean, remember the end of it?"

"How could I ever forget it?" Laura repeated, entirely serious this time.

"Yeah. You stumbled and grabbed onto me, and the way we were pressed together, I couldn't help showing you how much I wanted you. But you just stared at me for a long time and proceeded to make a joke. It was then that I remembered who I was, and who you were."

"What do you mean?" Laura demanded, awfully afraid

that Miguel knew about her father and was angry at her deception.

"I mean that I looked at your fine Wasp skin and saw my brown hand on it. It was then I remembered that I was a mixed-breed Mexican-Irish Indian who didn't know how to dance the fox-trot, or about a thousand other things that must be important to you."

Laura felt her mouth fall open and her eyes widen as Miguel revealed his innermost fears. Although she felt like weeping, when she buried her face into his chest her overflowing emotions for some reason were transformed into a soft, deep chuckle that shook her body.

"Laura, don't cry, sweetheart. It's not your fault, *querida*," he said, rocking her against himself. "I'm not angry with you."

Laura reveled in the comforting movement, until she succumbed to another wave of laughter.

Miguel suddenly held her out at arm's length. "Why you're not crying," he yelled. "You're giggling, you little witch. What in the hell? Laura!"

"Wasp?" she choked, "Wasp! Oh, darling, it just hit me how little we know about each other. I have to tell you a lot more about myself, and I definitely want to hear the fascinating circumstances that produced a Mexican-Irish Indian.

"Mexican, and Irish, and Indian," Laura repeated, shaking her head. "Well, one thing I already know. You obviously didn't inherit any of the fabled powers of your ancestors."

"I haven't got the slightest idea what you're talking about," Miguel protested.

"If you were the tiniest bit fey, or second-sighted, or whatever they call it, you would have understood just what was happening to me during that notorious dance we shared. Dearest one, I stepped all over your toes because I wanted to drag you off somewhere—and beg you to make love to me!"

"Make love! Even then?" He groaned. "Do you realize how many laps I had to run, how many cold showers I've had to take because of you? My God, we've wasted a year and a half of our lives!"

Miguel's mouth captured Laura's so suddenly that she didn't have time to take a breath. Lights flashed behind her eyelids, and her consciousness was about to depart before Miguel finally lifted his head.

"Laura, I can't let you go back to San Gabriel on Monday. We won't be able to see each other again until we finish our two-year commitment in July. That's almost three months. They've got to let us get married right away," he said, desperation roughening his voice.

"Right away?" Laura repeated.

"Why not? The Pfeiffers got permission, why not us?"

"Why not us? Why not us!" Laura felt that she was turning into a human echo. Then Miguel sealed her acceptance of their union in a slow, gentle, supremely sensual way, and she had no more room in her mind for anything except him.

She didn't learn any more about his family that night. And she never had a chance to tell him about hers, about her father. Instead, even though their physical limitations tempered its expression, she and Miguel spent the night proving their love for each other. They didn't sleep until dawn crept down the patchworked sides of Pichincha.

Even though they were exhausted, it was very early the next morning when the newly-engaged pair went to the Peace Corps office to find out how they could get married as soon as possible. They were lighthearted and laughing when they rushed into the building. But just inside the entry hall, Laura stopped so abruptly that Miguel almost ran into her.

Her eyes were snared by the three men coming out of the country director's office, heads bent in conversation. Laura let out a whoop, and dragging Miguel with her, she rushed toward the group.

"Papa! Papa, what are you doing here?" she shouted, letting go of Miguel's hand to throw herself into her father's arms.

"*Liebling, liebling*. Look at you—so pale, so thin! And my good friend, Robert Conroy, was just telling me that you were well again." He looked accusingly at the Peace Corps administrator.

Before the poor man could open his mouth, Laura was assuring her father of her return to good health.

"I'm fine, Papa. In fact, I can't remember when I ever felt better," she announced, turning her head around to grin at Miguel, who was looking back and forth between daughter and father with narrowed eyes.

It was obvious that Miguel recognized the face that had been on the cover of *Time* magazine last year. The face of Gustav Nordheim . . . physicist, scientific advisor to three presidents, and the chairman of the International Committee for the Safe Use of Nuclear Power.

"Laura, look who I've brought along to see you." Tugging on her hand, Laura's father pulled her attention away from Miguel's stunned features, and turned her toward the sandy-haired man waiting patiently next to Bob Conroy.

"I have to disagree with you, Gustav. Laura's never been more beautiful. She's glowing." Jerrold Easten, her father's administrative aide, held out his arms. Laura automatically went into the embrace of the man she had known since she was ten.

"Jerry, I'm glad to see you." Only a few inches taller than she, he wrapped her into an intense bear hug.

"I've missed you so much, Laura," he murmured into her ear, before kissing her lightly on the mouth.

Feeling a sudden, uncomfortable tingle on the back of her neck, Laura tugged away from Jerry's arms. She turned, wanting to introduce Miguel to her father. But her brand-new fiancé was no longer behind her. Neither was he anywhere else in the converted office building, even though she searched through every room.

She didn't know it at the time, but fifteen years, two months, eight hours and fourteen minutes of her life would flow away before Laura Nordheim Easten would see Miguel O'Brian again.

SIX

The grand lobby of the Sir Francis Drake Hotel glittered with man-made prisms of light. Enormous crystal chandeliers were reflected, again and again, in mirrors that scaled up the walls to the vaulted ceilings.

Any other time, Laura would have been left breathless by such beauty. Tonight, she sat in the lobby for more than a half hour, so lost in the past that her mind hardly registered a detail of the surrounding splendor.

A noisy influx of people abruptly jarred Laura back into the present. *Why am I waiting here,* she asked herself harshly? She'd be a fool to have a drink with Miguel O'Brian. What could they possibly have to say to each other after such a long time? More important, why had she ever agreed to meet with the man who had hurt her so badly?

What she should have done was go directly to her room and called home to see if Mai was feeling any better. Well, that was exactly what she was going to do now. But at least *she* would leave Miguel a message at the reception desk before disappearing from his life.

Unfortunately, there appeared to be at least two dozen people ahead of her, all clamoring for the attention of the clerks. Anxiously checking the lobby, Laura prayed that Miguel would be late, or fail to see her in this shifting mass of humanity.

As her head swung back toward the desk, Laura's attention was suddenly snared by a sign with her name printed on it. She did a classic double take, and then gave an embarrassed little laugh, belatedly realizing that the large block letters were part of a stand-up information board. It listed the hotel's schedule of events, which included her seminar.

With the lifelong habit of a compulsive reader, Laura automatically scanned the other activities that had been planned for the day.

It seemed that the fiftieth wedding anniversary of Mr. and Mrs. Thomas Gillis was being celebrated on the Starlite Roof. And in the Empire Room, the American Chemists' Society would be discussing the place of native herbs in modern medicine. Their keynote speaker was Michael O'Brian, Ph.D., explaining how he had discovered the wonder drug Cholchinase in South America. The Bank of the West's annual shareholders' meeting . . . *Michael O'Brian? Miguel?*

"There you are, Laura. Lord, it's a miracle I found you in this crowd." Miguel's murmur was low and husky in her ear, but it somehow penetrated the babel surrounding them.

Laura whirled, ready to give Miguel the smooth excuse she was going to leave for him at the reception desk. But there seemed to be some sort of breakdown in her nervous system. Try as she might, all she could do was look up in mute agony into Miguel's magnificent eyes.

She's tired, Michael thought. *Tired and confused, and God help me, so incredibly beautiful.* The promise of her youth had been more than fulfilled. Each feature was delicately perfect, cleanly etched, yet womanly soft. He couldn't help scanning down her body, his eyes trying to delve beneath the feminine version of an executive's suit.

Peeking out from business gray was a soft, peachy cloud of a blouse.

A smile tugged at the edges of Michael's mouth. Laura was probably unaware that the sensuously colored material, which demurely veiled the sweet swell of her firm breasts, also whispered that a passionate heart beat underneath those layers.

He had never forgotten her passion. And unfair as it was, even in the midst of his most serious relationships, he had been compelled to compare each woman to that memory—to a perfection that perhaps even the mature Laura couldn't match.

Someone bumped into Michael's shoulder, and he abruptly realized they were in the direct flow of traffic. "Would you like to go up the Starlite Roof on the twenty-first floor, Laura? There's music and dancing and a great view of the city."

"I'm not interested in music or dancing, Miguel, and anyway, a private party rented the room for an anniversary celebration." Laura was pleased that her voice sounded so cool, even if her words were a bit stilted.

Michael looked down on her for a long second. "Then I guess it's the Corporate Lounge. This way, Laura."

He exerted a gentle, yet inexorable, pressure on Laura's elbow when her eyes told him that she was about to bolt. He couldn't let her run away—not now, not yet.

As Laura allowed herself to be shepherded into the chandelier-lit room, her spine straightened with firm decision and the panic faded from her eyes. OK, she'd have a drink with him. She would be calm and mature. But she was going to ask Miguel O'Brian some tough questions. Even after fifteen years, Laura ached for the answers.

"What's your preference these days, Laura?" Michael asked, when they settled into huge, overstuffed chairs. "I'll bet it's something a little more sophisticated than the gallons of *café con leche* we used to drink in Ecuador."

His attempt at humor backfired. A vivid picture formed

in his mind of the toast they had made to each other with the sweet, milk-laced Ecuadorian coffee the last morning they had been together in Quito.

"A Margarita would be fine," Laura murmured to the cocktail hostess who had appeared to take their order.

She must not recall that salute to their future, Michael decided, relieved and yet angry at the same time because cursed with total recall, he could remember it—and every single moment they had spent together.

"What will you have, sir?"

"Scotch on the rocks." Michael practically snarled at the girl. Then, seeing the shock in the young woman's eyes, he added a few gently humorous words to soften his rudeness.

Almost against her will, Laura studied Miguel while he talked with the hostess. The young lady was actually blushing, although his end of the conversation was light and entirely proper.

Yet, the girl's eyes devoured his stark, uncompromising features. And Laura had to admit that the harsh harmony of his face projected a potent virility that was infinitely more compelling than mere handsomeness.

"So, when did you move to Los Angeles, Laura?"

Sometime in the last few seconds the girl had disappeared and Miguel had turned his attention back to Laura. Caught in the act of staring at him, she fought to dampen a blush of her own. At the same time, Laura struggled to retrieve whatever it was he had just said.

Seeing her confusion, Michael tried again. "I was asking how long you've lived in California."

"Oh . . . about three years. I moved to the West Coast just after my husband died," Laura blurted, revealing much more to Miguel than she would have if she had been paying better attention.

"Died! My God, I'm sorry, Laura, I didn't know t–that . . ." Michael stopped abruptly, clenching his shaking hands into fists under the table.

He never would have wished the man dead, but why hadn't he used the contacts he had developed in the last few years to keep track of Laura? If he hadn't given up hope, he could have found out where she lived and monitored how she was doing. Then he would have known that Jerrold Easten had been gone for three years. More than a year before Michael had met Kattie. And even five months ago, it wouldn't have been too late to . . .

"Your drinks, sir, madame." Not realizing the turbulent thoughts she was interrupting, the young waitress placed their order in front of the pair, smiled at Michael and then disappeared into the shadows.

For a few seconds, Laura traced a fingertip over the lace-like netting of salt that decorated her glass, watching Miguel swirl the chilled contents of his drink around and around. His body shifted restlessly, as if he'd dearly love to get up and pace.

Laura recalled an image of Miguel—seventeen years earlier, during Peace Corps training—struggling to contain that same driving energy while they sat through yet another long lecture. Pushing away the past, Laura tried to focus on her purpose for having this drink with him . . . information.

"Do you have something to do with Cholchinase, Miguel?" she asked, the end of her pink-tipped finger still following a salty trail around her glass.

Michael's head snapped up, momentarily thrown by Laura's non sequitur. "Ah, yes, I do. I discovered it and I formed a research company to work out the purification process."

"So, you *were* the keynote speaker at that chemists' meeting this evening," she confirmed, more to herself than to him. Then she lifted challenging eyes. "Maybe I should call you Michael from now on. Why did you change your name?"

Even in the dim light, Laura could see the flush that spread across his high cheekbones.

"It seemed to make things easier when I was starting my firm," Michael finally answered. "People were more . . . comfortable with the Irishman. It saved answering a lot of irrelevant questions about the Mexican and Indian parts of me."

"People were more comfortable? Don't you mean that *you* were? Hasn't the change cost you a great deal of yourself, like three-quarters of your heritage, *Michael*?"

Illogically, her use of his anglicized name angered him. "Look, Laura, just go on calling me Miguel," he said, trying to appear casual. "But don't be so smug. How could you ever understand what I faced?"

"Gosh, you're right. How very rude of me. What you call yourself is absolutely none of my business." The blatant insincerity of her apology was evident to both of them.

"No, it's none of your business," Michael bit off. "What do you know of prejudice, Laura? Laura of the blond hair and white skin."

"Not much, except that it killed every one of my relatives on my father's side. And he only survived because his parents managed to bribe enough officials to smuggle him out of Nazi Germany in 1938."

"Your father?" Michael shook his head, hardly able to take in what she was saying.

"Yes, you remember my father, Gustav Nordheim. You met him in Ecuador. Oh, that's right. You didn't stay long enough to be formally introduced, did you? You magically vanished in front of a whole roomful of people. You know, I've always wondered how you got out of the building so fast. I searched everywhere . . ."

Laura abruptly stopped. *So much for calm maturity*, she mocked herself. Taking a deep breath, she tried to reorganize her thoughts. "Look, Miguel, even after fifteen years, I wouldn't be normal if I still wasn't a bit curious. I know I threw myself at you back then, but there was no need for you to run off like that. I certainly wouldn't have gotten my dad to go after you with a shotgun when you had second thoughts. You could have just told me it was a mistake.''

"God, Laura, I never thought that my feelings for you were a mistake. But when I saw who your father was, and when that guy in the Ivy League suit kissed you like he had every right, I must have gone into shock. And to answer one of your questions, to this day I don't even remember leaving that building. One minute I was with you and the next thing I knew, I was sitting on a bus loaded with farmers and their chickens.''

"Miguel, that's ridiculous . . .'' Laura began. But he didn't seemed to hear her and continued talking.

"I was halfway up the aisle, ready to ask the driver to stop, when I realized that I needed some time to think. Time to decide if I had anything to offer the daughter of Gustav Nordheim.''

Laura made an inarticulate sound of protest, unable to form the words that could express the anger she felt. She sat in silent rage, watching Miguel run a shaking hand through his straight, black hair and then lean forward.

"I knew that I couldn't give you the wealth or the mansion you were used to,'' he continued. "Not to mention the glamour that went with your life. I was scared to death that after the first glow of attraction wore off, you'd be more comfortable with somebody like the man who was with your father. I didn't know if my loving you until the day I died would be enough to . . .''

"Love? Love!'' Laura was finally able to sputter. "No. What you felt was just lust. A man in love wouldn't have left me like that, without a word, without a good-bye. Didn't you think about how frightened I would be, and then how ashamed? My father and Jerry thought I was crazy, searching the Peace Corps headquarters, room by room. I kept running back and forth to the pensione, questioning anyone I thought might have seen you.''

Raucous laughter interrupted Laura's tirade. Looking

around, she saw that the lounge had filled up. Their table was no longer an isolated island of privacy.

Muttering a ladylike curse, Laura lowered the volume of her voice, while increasing its level of sarcasm. "But now I finally understand what happened. You *loved* me so much that you decided to give me up. I can just hear you telling the farmers and chickens, 'Tis a far, far better thing I do today, then I have ever done before . . .' What rot!"

"Laura, it wasn't like . . ." Michael tried to interrupt.

"No!" She put up a small, silencing hand. "At least let me finish. It's a little late, Miguel, but I'll describe the wonderful life of Gustav Nordheim's daughter. A mansion? We lived in a two-bedroom apartment, and not at the Watergate, I can assure you. Money? My father had a professor's salary, augmented by the magnificent royalties his books on physics earned. The prestige? Well, yes, he *was* famous.

"Three presidents consulted him on every scientific decision they made, and he was known around the world as an advocate of nuclear sanity. But me? To me, being his daughter just meant that I had a father who wasn't home an awful lot. Oh, yes, it also meant I had to live up to his reputation as a certified genius. That was loads of fun when my IQ is not at that level!"

Laura paused to take a deep drink of her Margarita, only to choke on the potent liquid. Struggling to recover her breath, she defiantly glared at Miguel, daring him to laugh. But he just sat there, looking a little stunned, allowing her the opportunity to finish her monologue—to finish with her yesterdays.

"Ah, it was a very exciting life I led. But it was also a very sheltered one. So, perhaps I should thank you for breaking off our very short engagement. Because after that episode with you, I was able to recognize *mature* love when Jerry—that guy in the Ivy League suit—asked me to marry him."

Seeing the sudden look of pain in Miguel's eyes, Laura wanted to bite her tongue off for that cheap shot. Instead, she quickly retrieved her purse and briefcase and got up. She had to leave before she revealed exactly how long it had taken for her to admit that Miguel was never coming back, and finally say yes to Jerry's repeated proposals.

Miguel also stood up, filling Laura's universe with the breadth of his shoulders.

"Laura, you can't go like this. You're right, my first impulse back then was immature. But for God's sake, remember that I *was* immature then. We both were very young for our age.

"I'd like to think I'd handle a situation like that a lot better, if it happened today. And from what I saw of your lecture this afternoon, I know that you've matured beautifully. Laura, show me some of the compassion and empathy I sensed in you today. Please sit down again. Listen to the rest of my story."

Miguel's deep voice was quiet, yet so compelling that Laura couldn't move. They stood staring at each other until Laura finally acknowledged the subtle combination of sincerity and manipulation in his request with a wry little smile.

Sighing, she settled back into her chair. Her arms, however, still clutched her belongings to her breast, as if their fine leather construction would shield her from anything else Miguel might say.

"All right, Miguel, go on. You were telling me about your magical, mystery bus ride when I interrupted you."

Miguel smiled a wide grin that Laura's briefcase did absolutely nothing to deflect. She felt as if her blood had caught fire and her galloping heart was pumping the blaze to the most vulnerable parts of her body.

"Oh, in reality, there wasn't anything mysterious about it, Laura. The farmers and chickens and I were on an express bus to Otavalo."

Miguel's face gradually became serious and his gaze

turned inward. Laura managed to gain control of her racing pulse by the time he continued.

"It was Saturday. So, when I got to the town, I spent the day wandering the market. I walked between the stalls, hardly seeing the ponchos and woodcarvings and Panama hats that were for sale. I think I was making some sort of mental ledger, trying to balance what I could give you against the kind of life you led."

Before the indignation that sparked in Laura's eyes could reach her mouth, Michael put up a calming hand.

"The kind of life I *thought* you led." He grinned, watching the light of battle recede from her eyes. *What a beautiful little volcano she is*, Michael thought as Laura sat back in her chair. Her righteous indignation was another hint of the passion simmering just beneath that lovely pale skin. What he wouldn't give to feel that softness under him, to tap into that fire.

God, what was he thinking! He had no right to covet her, absolutely none.

"Miguel, what's wrong? Are you ill?" Laura asked softly. There was an expression of loss on his lean face that made her want to put her arms around him, to rock him like she used to rock with Mai before her daughter had gotten too prickly for comforting.

Mai! Oh, she had to get out of here. Miguel was making her forget her priorities.

"Miguel, I'm sorry to interrupt, but I have to go now. I've got things that I have to do . . ."

Jarred out of his guilty agony, Michael dealt with Laura's declaration by ignoring it. He plowed back into the past before she could move.

"I was telling you about that ledger I was visualizing. On the positive side, I knew that nobody else would ever love you like I did. And once I had time to think about it, I also realized that my being poor didn't have to be a permanent condition. With hard work and some brains, there was no reason why I couldn't make something of myself. Then I remembered the night we had spent together and decided that only a fool would throw away what we had.

"But, by the time I got things into perspective, the last bus to Quito had left and I had to spend the night. When I finally got back late the next morning and went to the pensione, someone else was in your room. At the Peace Corps office, they told me you'd returned to San Gabriel already, a day ahead of schedule."

"Of course, I did. I had nothing to stay for. My father and Jerry left a few hours after you did. They'd only stopped to check up on my health on their way to a conference in Lima. And after calling all the hospitals and the police, it was obvious that foul play was not involved. You had disappeared because you wanted to disappear. I felt like such a fool. Getting out of Quito was all I could think of."

Her words were belligerent, but a picture formed in her mind of their buses passing each other that Sunday morning, going in opposite directions on the cobblestone paving of the Pan American Highway.

"Shades of Thomas Hardy." Michael smiled wryly, somehow reading her mind.

"Star-crossed lovers, you mean? Oh, I'm afraid that doesn't wash, Miguel. If you'd really come back, planning to marry me, why didn't I ever hear from you again? I know you had to go into the Oriente to help out when that volcano blew up—when Antisana erupted—but after the crisis was over, why didn't you contact me? The other Volunteers got back a month before our two-year tour was up, but not you."

The grin slipped from Michael's lips. "No, not me. Laura, you've got to believe me, I did write. And I didn't come back with the others because I was persuaded to stay on in the Oriente." His eyes lifted to the ceiling. "Can't you hear them, Laura?"

"Hear whom, Miguel?" Puzzled, her gaze followed

his, but she only saw the ornate molding decorating the plaster.

"Why, the *Kachinas*, the Pueblo spirits my mother worships. Listen, they're up there, laughing at me even now. Over the years, they've literally moved heaven and earth to keep us apart, Laura."

"Miguel? You don't really believe what you're saying, do you?" Laura whispered, and then silently asked herself just what did she know about this man? Had he gone 'round the bend? Anything could have happened to him in fifteen years. "You can't blame something like that on mythical gods. No, it was your decision to stay away, a decision you made of your own free will."

"Free will. Ah, Laura, t'ain't no such animal." He turned an ear upward. "Lord, they're loud tonight, honey."

Laura didn't know if it was her fear that Miguel was mad, or if it was the impact of that sweet word on her heart, but she could feel tears smarting behind her eyelids.

Michael immediately relented when he saw the telltale sheen in her huge brown eyes. "I'm sorry, Laura, I didn't mean to frighten you. You're right, I don't really believe in divine retribution. At least, Michael O'Brian, the thirty-eight-year-old scientist knows that he isn't being hounded by mocking *Kachinas*.

"Although I have to admit that sometimes the six-year-old Miguel Enrique Vincente peeks out from his place in my memory. And that boy reminds me of all the Pueblo stories his mother told him about the *yiapana* and what those winter witches would do to him if he misbehaved, or questioned, or disbelieved."

"Miguel, please," Laura protested, "this isn't getting us anywhere."

"Oh, yes, it is. I'm trying to tell you what happened when I got back to Quito. I was all set to follow you to San Gabriel on Monday. But don't you remember exactly when Antisana blew?"

Laura shook her head, mutely imploring him to get done with his story. All this rehashing of the past was getting to be too painful.

"On that same Monday, at four in the morning."

"Oh, yes," Laura murmured. "All those people killed, the lava, the earthquakes, the landslides. When I heard about it, I volunteered to go help with the cleanup, too. But Mr. Conroy wouldn't let me leave San Gabriel. He said that I hadn't recovered enough yet."

"Well, I guess he thought dog bites healed faster than appendectomies because Conroy jumped at my request."

"Yes, I know. I can't remember who it was, but somebody passing through town stopped at the house where I was living and told me that he saw you going off with a half dozen other volunteers in a Peace Corps Jeep."

"Yeah, we threw some supplies together and left on Monday afternoon. Two days later, I was in a mud-covered town at the headwaters of the Amazon, digging houses and cattle and people out of the muck. We worked twenty hours a day for weeks. We did nothing but shovel and sleep, and then get up to work some more."

Staring at him now, Laura recalled the mixed emotions she had felt when she learned that Miguel had gone into the Oriente. She had been relieved that he was alive, yet angry that he hadn't come after her, or at least tried to contact her. But, as the weeks went by, she had grown more and more fearful for his safety in the volcano-ravaged region where Ecuador, Peru, and Brazil blended together into the upper Amazon jungle.

Michael abruptly reached across the table. He calmly disposed of Laura's bag and briefcase shield to claim control of her hands. Gripping them tightly, he spoke with undeniable sincerity.

"Laura, in spite of having total recall, *that* whole time is just a muddled haze in my memory. Perhaps it was a defense against all the horror. Yet, there's one thing that I do remember. I wrote you to let you know what had happened, and to tell you that I loved you with all my heart."

"No, no, no," she murmured.

"You must believe me," Michael urged when he heard Laura's soft words of denial. "I sent you a note before leaving Quito. I begged you to forgive me and to let me have another chance when I returned. Over the months that followed, I wrote at least a dozen letters, saying much the same, but I never got your answer."

"No! *I* was the one who wrote," Laura insisted, "and I never heard from you! When I found out where you were, and got over my initial anger, I sent several letters in care of the Peace Corps headquarters. I asked Mr. Conroy to relay them to you because I heard that the mail service had been cut off to the Oriente."

Michael gave a significant glance upward, and then laughed shortly. "OK, if not 'them,' then I guess somebody else was against us. I said that I never got your answer, and I didn't, because none of our letters were forwarded! Laura, when I finally got back to Quito, all of our correspondence to each other was in a neat pile, with my luggage and books."

"How could that happen? It's illegal to interfere with letters!"

"In the U.S., perhaps. Anyway, nobody could explain the mixup. One of the secretaries at the Peace Corps office said she found them in a storage cabinet. She was looking for supplies for the new director after Mr. Conroy left to take a consular post in England. She decided to put all of them with my things.

"God, I was frustrated. Those letters were proof that you still cared for me, but I had no way of contacting you. You had left for the States already and I didn't know your home address."

With a quick, angry jerk of her hands, Laura managed to pull away from Miguel's grasp.

"Ah, Miguel, you just blew it! Here I was, almost

beginning to believe you. But like most liars, you just had to take your little fairytale one step too far, buddy.''

"Liar! What are you talking about?''

"When I realized you weren't going to get back before I left, I wrote my home address and phone number in my last letter. I even told Mr. Conroy the information was enclosed and to make sure you got it.'' Laura glared at him, daring him to deny the truth of that.

"That one wasn't with those I got,'' he protested vehemently. "And when I tried to get the information from the Peace Corps, your address turned out to be one of the best-kept secrets in the country. Because of your father, I was told. The only clue I had was that you lived in a Maryland suburb of Washington, D.C. I remembered you telling me that on the first day we met. I thought about walking up and down streets and knocking on doors until I found you.''

"You remembered something I said to you from that first day?'' Laura whispered, trying not to soften.

"*Querida*, as I said a minute ago, I have total recall . . . but even if I didn't, I couldn't forget a single thing about you. You were in my thoughts every day for years.'' He regained her hands and then rested his forehead against her trembling fingers for a long moment.

"Then what kept you from your walking tour of greater Washington?'' Laura demanded quietly.

He slowly raised his beautiful eyes to hers. "Two years in the Army, which I spent in one of those unnamed military actions in Central America.''

"Oh, Miguel! They drafted you? Even after the Peace Corps, after doing all that rescue work?''

"Yeah, at the risk of sounding completely paranoid, I think somebody, somewhere, must have liked me,'' he grinned sardonically and then sighed. "Well, maybe they did because I survived another, darker jungle. And even in Ecuador—when Conroy kept asking me to go deeper and deeper into the Amazon region—I not only survived,

I also found something that eventually led to a Ph.D. and a successful research company.''

''Cholchinase,'' Laura breathed, remembering the information sign in the lobby.

''That's right. The last tribe I worked with used a primitive form of the drug. They shared their knowledge with me, and I ended up with a patent for a medicine that's helping thousands of people with angina clean out their clogged blood vessels. But that was much later, after I got back from the Army. And after I found out that you had married Jerrold Easten.''

''Miguel, I'm sorry for what I said a few minutes ago. It was just plain cruel,'' Laura whispered. ''I didn't jump into marriage. My wedding was more than two years after I left Ecuador. I kept refusing Jerry until my father got so . . . Until Papa retired from the university.''

Why was she telling him all this, Laura suddenly wondered. How long she had put Jerry off, waiting for Miguel to contact her, didn't matter now. And what good would it do anyone to talk about all the nights she had been plagued by anxiety dreams about him?

''God, Laura, you see what I mean. The fates were against us.''

''Yes, maybe they were. Against you and me, I mean. But I had a happy marriage, and I won't lie to you and say that I'm sorry about my years with Jerry. I loved him and I love the daughter he gave me.''

''Daughter! You have a daughter?''

''Yes, Mai. She's eleven, and very . . . special.'' Laura grinned at Miguel, unable to keep the glow of maternal pride from lighting her eyes. ''She's been trying to choose between taking a doctorate in math or becoming a concert violinist.''

''At eleven?''

''Well, we've decided that it's best for her to go to the local junior high next year, but she already has enough college credits to enter any university as a sophomore.''

"Whew, and here I was thinking that Jeff was precocious."

"Jeff?" Laura asked, a line of puzzlement between her eyes.

"Oh, a neighbor's kid," Michael said, feeling his cheeks begin to burn.

But Laura didn't seem to notice. She had picked up her belongings again and stood up. Her next words made him forget all about Jeff, or even Kattie—for the moment.

"I really have to go, Miguel. Mai had a bad cold coming on when I left Los Angeles this morning, so I want to go up to my room and call home to see how she is."

"Well, I can certainly understand your concern. I'll walk you to your room."

He quickly threw some money on the table, and before she could react he had gotten up and captured her hand again, lacing his fingers together with hers.

Appalled by the heat his skin radiated against her palm, Laura tried to think of some excuse to get away from him.

"This isn't necessary," she argued. "I'm just on the third floor."

"All the more reason for me to check your room out. Thieves go to the lower floors first, you know. I won't feel comfortable until I hear you bolt your door."

So, hand in hand, they went to the elevator. Michael nodded politely to the other people getting on with them, smiling to himself while the compartment filled up and Laura was forced to mold her body closer to his.

She breathed a sigh of relief when he finally let her hand go. But then, Miguel slung his arm around her shoulder and began to wind a lock of her long hair around an index finger.

Laura was very grateful that the first stop was hers. As soon as the doors opened, she all but burst out of the elevator. Miguel went right with her, his fingers still buried under the heavy fall of her hair.

Although she knew it was impossible, Laura imagined

that each separate strand had come alive and that her contrary hair had wrapped around Miguel's hand, seeking to ensnare him so he could never get away from her again.

The whimsical fantasy cleared right out of her head, as Laura neared her room and heard the strident ring of her telephone. Running the last few feet, she quickly unlocked the door and rushed into the room.

Michael hesitated in the doorway and then entered, quietly closing the door behind him. He saw that Laura was pacing nervously, pressing the phone receiver to her ear. He listened intently to her side of the conversation.

"Yes, Marthe, I'm here. Please slow down. *Auf Englisch, bitte, auf Englisch!* Have you given her any medication? Why don't you make that acetaminophen, instead of aspirin, if she gets up again. No, don't wake her. It's better if she sleeps. But we don't want this to get out of control. I'll cancel the rest of my appointments and be home on the first plane in the morning. The doctor will probably want to prescribe another round of antibiotics. Now, get some rest yourself. No, you don't have to sit up with her. *Schlafst du, Marthe, schlafst du!* And don't worry, I'm sure Mai will be fine by tomorrow."

Breaking the connection, she immediately contacted her boss and explained the situation. John Stewart, the father of three, told her not to worry and that he would reschedule her appointments for later in the month. Thanking him for his understanding, she then called the airline and managed to get a seat on the nine o'clock plane.

Finally replacing the receiver on its cradle, Laura absently began rubbing her forehead. The biting tension between her eyes hurt so much that she felt like crying. Laura didn't know Miguel had come up behind her, until his strong fingers added a healing pressure to the back of her neck.

"How sick is your daughter?" he asked.

"She has an earache and a sore throat. It could be the

beginning of another strep infection. She had a couple during the spring.''

Worried as she was, Laura felt the tension seep out of her as Miguel continued his ministrations. She leaned back against his warmth, allowing his strength to support her for a luxurious second.

"I'm sure she'll be OK. Kids get these things a lot."

"I know, but I can't take any chances with her. She's all I've got left, Miguel. E—everyone else is gone."

Unexpectedly, the tears she had been fighting broke through and began to drizzle down her cheeks. Even as she let go and really began to sob, one detached part of her brain tried to analyze why she was giving such a free rein to emotions she had held in check so long.

Maybe it was because she felt so natural, so safe in Miguel's arms, Laura told herself. Or perhaps it was because it had been so long since she'd had anyone to talk to, ages since she had been able to share even a fraction of her worry with someone she loved.

Loved? No, that was no longer true. *Had* loved, perhaps. And, of course, she still liked Miguel—respected him—now that she understood what really had happened in Ecuador. But loved? No!

Even while she was denying her feelings, Miguel suddenly leaned down and swept her up into his arms. He strode to the easy chair next to a writing desk.

Before she could protest, Laura was stretched across his thighs. He placed her arms around his neck and began rocking her as if she were a child. She reveled in the rare feeling of being comforted and cosseted. As his soothing voice murmured soft words of encouragement in her ear, Laura just cried and cried.

Sometime later, when the tears she had been damming up for years finally dried, she wiped her cheeks and blew her nose on the large white handkerchief Miguel magically produced from somewhere.

"Feeling better, sweetheart?" he asked, smiling at the wide, childlike expression in her eyes.

"Yes, thank you. I am feeling much better now, Miguel. But I want you to know that I don't do this very often." She sniffled once more.

Michael grinned again, taking the wet linen from her hand to make a last, efficient sweep at the moisture remaining on her cheeks.

"You're very good at that. Have you practiced on your own kids' tears?"

"No kids, Laura."

"Are you married, Miguel?"

"I've never been married, Laura. There wasn't time at first, and then, well . . ." It was the truth—as far as it went.

Tell her the rest, you bastard, don't let this go on. But Laura touched his cheek with warm fingers just then. She brushed an errant strand of hair back into place, and Michael found that he couldn't utter another word.

"Haven't you ever wanted a family, Miguel?"

"Oh, yes, quite desperately at times, Laura. Especially in the last few years."

There, it wasn't more than a husky whisper, but he wasn't mute. However, instead of saying what he should have said, someone else took over his vocal chords, someone who directed the casual words that came out next.

"Tell me more about Mai. What does she look like, this daughter of yours?"

"Well, if you let me off your lap, I'll get my purse and show you a complete collection of photos since the day she was born."

"No, just describe her in your own words, Laura." Michael didn't want to let her go, and he didn't want to see pictures that might include her husband. Somehow, he felt that man had stolen something that should have been his: all those years with Laura, and a child of his own seed.

"Of course, I think that Mai Lin is the most beautiful young lady in the whole world," Laura was saying.

"Mai Lin, that's a lovely name. Unusual, sounds almost . . ."

"Oriental?" Laura laughed.

"Yes, I guess."

"That's because she was named for my mother."

"What?"

"Mai Lin Olsen was her maiden name. She met my father in New York, at her Carnegie debut as a concert violinist. But she originally came from Hawaii. She was part Chinese and Norwegian, and a little bit of everything else!"

Laura had to smile at the stunned expression on Miguel's face. "Oh yes, Miguel Enrique Vincente O'Brian, *I'm* as much a part of the American melting pot as you are. That's another thing we never had a chance to discuss in Ecuador. Something else we had in common."

"Oh, Laura, I was so stupid, so self-centered back then. I thought nobody else could have had the mixed-up background I felt I was cursed with."

"A curse, oh, no, Miguel. How can it be a curse when my child is absolutely beautiful, with clear blue eyes, set at an exotic angle? And how can mixing genes be wrong when she inherited every IQ point my father and Jerry had, along with the exceptional musical ability of my mother? Don't you remember the rule about hybrid strength?"

"You mean that the offspring is often finer than the parents?"

"Exactly! Mai is a marvelous example of that. You and I would have had just as wonderful . . ." Laura clapped a censoring hand over her betraying mouth.

"Yes, *querida*, you're right, our children would have been truly fantastic." Lifting her hand away from her lips, Miguel kissed her fingers, before placing them against his chest.

There, Laura felt the strong beat of his heart. Without thinking about her actions, she quickly released enough buttons so that her fingers could slip inside Miguel's shirt. She desperately needed to feel the life-giving rhythm directly against her own skin.

Before she could take another breath, Miguel's arms went around her, crushing her to his body. Her hand was trapped over a heart that had doubled its rate in a fraction of a second. Then, for the first time in fifteen years, he took her mouth.

An invading tongue thrust between her pliant lips, and Laura once again tasted an essence she had never quite forgotten.

A moan escaped her throat as the kiss deepened and deepened. Hands frantically searched and provoked and measured. For long minutes, Laura's sighs of pleasure were matched by Miguel's groans of need. And then, mechanical sounds dominated the room for a few seconds.

A zipper whirred down, a belt buckle clanked open and various pieces of clothing fell onto deep, rich carpeting. An instant later, the bed's wide, firm mattress protested faintly when two fused bodies tumbled onto it.

After that, the only sounds that mattered were again beautifully human. Their need was too great to exchange the little jokes and laughter that would have been part of their loving, if they hadn't lost long years. But there were urgent whispers and gasped phrases of surprise and praise. Finally, the sweetest sound of all echoed around the room: the barely recognizable blending of each other's names when the tumult came upon them.

Laura thought that she had shed her last tears into Miguel's handkerchief, but in the wake of an ecstasy she had not thought possible—a merging of body and mind and soul she had never dreamed of—she found herself sobbing again onto his smooth, hard chest.

Those hot tears abruptly pulled Michael back from the

incredibly high pinnacle where Laura's lovemaking had sent him. Afraid that he was crushing her with his heavy body, Michael made a halfhearted attempt to relieve her of his weight. Laura's arms and legs instantly tightened around him.

"No, stay in me! Don't leave me," she demanded fiercely.

"I won't go, I can't," Michael whispered in a voice that was clotted with tears of his own. There was no place on earth he would rather be than buried in the sweet, warm glove of her body.

The emotion is his voice shocked Laura enough to stop her weeping. When Miguel finally raised his head, she saw that his eyes were as wet as her own.

"I've been starving, Laura," he whispered. "All this time, and I never knew that I was slowly dying from the lack of you."

God, what could she say to that? That she felt the same? That her long years with Jerry had meant so little in comparison with the few short months and days and minutes she had spent with Miguel? That was too awful to think, let alone say out loud! Yet, Miguel deserved to know what place he had always had in her heart.

"Darling, you were my first lover. I was a virgin on my wedding night, but I had already given you that gift in every sense, except the technical one. And for years after I married, every time I made love with my husband, I felt unfaithful . . . to *you*! I loved Jerry, I really did. He was a fine, wonderfully gentle man, but I still missed you. Thank heaven, we've found each other again."

Miguel squeezed his eyes tightly together. He seemed to be in great pain, as if her words had hurt, rather than caressed. What had she said to cause that reaction?

With a low moan, Laura dropped kisses down his neck and across his chest, trying to salve the incomprehensible agony he radiated.

Just when she was beginning to feel desperate, her lips

and tongue and fingertips seemed to break through the strange barrier Miguel had erected between them.

Slowly, seemingly against his will, Miguel's hands began stroking tantalizing lines down her back. Then his mouth came to life, moving over hers, tracing a moist trail along her upper lip, from edge to edge. And finally plunging inside, hot and cat-rough, his tongue incited hers into an erotic battle.

After a sweet eternity of those kisses, Miguel turned onto his back and pulled Laura across his hard frame. He captured her head in his hands and just looked at her for the longest time. His extraordinary green eyes were blazing so brightly that Laura felt the heat of them all over her face.

"Laura, whatever happens tomorrow, try to remember this moment, this night. You must believe me when I say that you are my only love. *Te quiero, Tu, mi amadora. Tu, tu, tu!*"

Miguel's vows of love pierced her with such power that Laura felt a surge of fire divide her depths, as strongly as if he were already buried within her.

"Oh, my darling," she said in a shaky voice, "I think you were right. The gods were keeping us apart when we were young. Perhaps they were testing us, testing our commitment to each other. But they've relented, haven't they, darling? Now we can be together—always!"

Her hand boldly captured his manhood, measuring his arousal and finding him thickly ready for her again.

Michael couldn't contain the words that burst from him, telling Laura just how much he needed her and exactly what he wanted her to do. She laughed wickedly, delighted with the response she had evoked.

The musical, sensual lilt of it danced around the room, as she straddled Miguel and incorporated his throbbing flesh deeply into the welcoming cradle of her love.

The wild groan he uttered, when the first rush of an incredible climax swamped Michael's senses, was not entirely because of that pleasure. It was partly for the agony which would come in the morning, for both of them.

He would love Laura until his last day on earth, but this was the only night they could ever have together.

Yet, although Laura would hate him—and although he would despise himself at dawn—nothing could have stopped him from having these hours with her. He needed these memories to last him a lifetime.

But he would have to pay for it in the morning, with an image that would haunt him to the grave. He knew that he would never forget the look on Laura's face when he told her about Kattie. Sweet, funny Kattie Sinclair, the woman he was going to marry next month.

SEVEN

Laura was definitely a morning person. Each day she would automatically wake up at five, jump out of bed and dash for the shower. Then, before anyone else began to stir, she'd do a few of the chores every working mother has to fit into her "spare" time.

The travel clock on the nearby table read just after five now. *No bounding out of bed for me today,* Laura thought, a slow, satisfied smile curving over her lips. She couldn't even move! Miguel had thrown a hard-muscled leg over her thighs. And while one arm held her around the waist, the fingers of his other hand were buried in her hair, cradling her head against the warm skin of his chest.

Laura had never felt so protected, or so desired. She gloried in the possessiveness of his embrace, remembering how his powerful body had melded with hers time after time last night. The thought sent an intense sensual thrill rushing through her.

She would never forget what they had shared all through the night. And somehow, waking up in Miguel's arms again, after fifteen years, didn't shock her as much as it should have. Perhaps it was because she had dreamed of being held like this, of caressing his hot, copper-colored skin, untold times over those years.

During her marriage she had dreaded the dreams, fought the memories. Especially after Jerry became ill, whenever she experienced the recurring fantasy, Laura felt very angry with her wayward subconscious.

This morning, she understood the deep sense of loss that had nibbled at the edges of her life. She knew that her love for Miguel O'Brian had always been buried within her. Even though she had believed he betrayed her in Ecuador, she continued to long for him, in spite of that misconception.

Yet, she had been happy with Jerry. It had taken him two years after her return from South America, but Jerrold Easten finally won her over with his cheerful and persistent wooing.

By the time she agreed to marry him, Laura had loved her father's assistant. Yet, in truth, no matter how valiantly she fought their pull when awake, her most erotic flights of fancy had always featured another man.

Laura felt her eyes fill with tears at the thought of her mental infidelity. She knew that Jerry hadn't suspected, and that if had he lived, she never would have left him . . . even if Miguel had come to her in daylight, in the flesh.

But now Jerry was gone, and she was weeping one more time for his pain, for the long struggle he had lost. She had fought every inch of the way with him. And when he had become too weak, she had fought *for* him: for every proven treatment, for every experimental drug—and finally—for the dignity of a pain-free passing.

Using the edge of the sheet to wipe away the salty flow that stung her eyes, Laura knew that her tears were really a good-bye. Three years after his death, she was finally able to say farewell and Godspeed to Jerry.

He would want her to get on with her life. And now she didn't have to be ashamed of her dreams anymore.

Ironically, that thought brought a hot blush to her cheeks. She had experienced *reality* with Miguel last night, and she knew that those years of fantasy paled by comparison.

But what about Miguel? Had he ever dreamed about her? After last night, would he want to share her future? Could a man who had reached thirty-eight, free and unentangled, want anything to do with a widow and her troubled, pre-adolescent daughter?

Laura moved her head slightly to examine his strong features. Even in sleep, there was no hint of vulnerability to soften those uncompromising bones, that wide, incredibly sensuous mouth. And though he must be exhausted after the energy he had brought to their lovemaking, the aura of restless vitality he projected when awake was hardly dimmed while he slumbered.

She watched his eyes make darting movements under his closed lids and his jaw muscles flex. Cocooned as she was in his warm embrace, Laura realized that even in sleep his metabolism burned high, sending his heated blood zipping to every inch of this long, perfectly molded male body.

Fascinated by the force that seemed to radiate from Miguel, she spread her fingers over and down his back, trying to measure the heat, to quantify his warmth. Her investigation soon lost its clinical nature, when her breath quickened and her own temperature soared.

Oh, how she loved his smooth skin and the leashed strength under its burnished covering. He had held her fiercely last night, and the power latent in his muscles should have frightened her. Yet, even when he had been lost in a shattering climax, he had made sure that his calloused hands did her no harm and that the hard thrust of his body only brought her a pleasure that matched his own.

No, she never had to fear that Miguel would hurt her physically. But she was well aware that he possessed the ability to wreak lasting devastation on her emotions. All through the night he told her how much he loved her, with words and with his body. Yet, he had done the same thing in Ecuador, and then he had deserted her the next morning.

Her troubling thoughts were forgotten a second later when Laura's wandering fingers encountered a jagged ridge marring the perfection of Miguel's thigh. She abruptly remembered the Ecuadorian hospital and a wide bandage covering this same area. As dawn brightened her hotel room, she lightly traced the three-inch scar the dog's teeth had caused.

"Hey, no fair touching mine, unless you let me examine yours, too," a deep, husky voice chided Laura.

She instantly jerked her fingers away from his leg. But Miguel's hand was already on her flat stomach, unerringly finding the evidence of her appendectomy. Before she even had time for embarrassment, Miguel had given the thin white line an affectionate caress and then he captured her mouth in a hot and moist good-morning kiss.

"Ah, *querida*, do you know that you are in grave danger of being made love to again?" he said, when he finally lifted his mouth from hers.

"Oh, I certainly hope so," Laura sighed, the comical catch in her voice only half planned.

Michael almost groaned when her gaze met his and he saw the honest desire in those golden-brown irises. She raised her arms in welcome, and his attention was immediately snared by the pert rise of rounded breasts that seemed to call for his devotion.

But his lips had barely grazed the velvet of her nipple when he pulled his head back, remembering that no matter how much he wanted it, he could not make love to Laura again.

Not until he talked to her and had a chance to clear up the shameful mess he had made of things. Lord, he couldn't believe what he had done last night! Instead of being open and forthright about his situation, he had made love to Laura, all the while letting her believe that he was a free man.

Even after the first time, he had compounded his sin by taking her over and over again. Time after time, he had been compelled to nuzzle Laura out of her sleep, whispering to her of love, stroking her until she opened herself to him and accepted his thrusting need once more.

The last time it happened, it only took a few short minutes for Laura's responsive body to provoke him into a climax of such incredible intensity that he actually blacked out. When he regained his scattered wits, Michael saw by the dazed look in Laura's eyes that she had found the same sort of ecstasy in his arms.

She had run trembling fingers over his features, as if committing his face into memory. Then, with a lingering kiss and beguiling smile, she slid back into an exhausted sleep.

Proud as he was that he had given Laura such pleasure, and as fulfilled as his own body had been, Michael's conscience hadn't let him follow her example. Instead, he had lain awake, remembering the promises he had made to another woman, the vow to marry Kattie Sinclair and to take care of her family.

He asked himself over and over, how could he have let all of them down so badly? Chasing behind that thought had been a second question: what in the world was he going to do now?

He must have dozed off with those turbulent thoughts swirling in his brain and slept fitfully until Laura's soft touch on his thigh had woken him a minute ago.

Michael realized that his subconscious had been working, even while he slept, because now things were very clear in his mind.

First of all, he knew that he would never marry anyone but Laura. How could he marry another woman, having found out that his love for Laura had never died? Thinking about it, he must have known that his engagement to Kattie was over yesterday, the minute he saw Laura again.

Of course, he would always be there if Kattie or her kids needed him—but only as a friend—not as a husband or stepfather. Somehow, Michael felt that Kattie would understand and wish him well.

Yet, he could hardly call her up this morning in Arkansas and say, "Hi, Kathryn, guess who I ran into last night . . . the woman I've really been in love with for the last seventeen years . . " No, he would have to wait until she returned and he could speak to her in person.

When Laura touched his shoulder, communicating her silent confusion, Michael finally remembered that he had been poised over her for a long minute while his mind churned out its revelations.

Looking down into her trusting eyes, he suddenly was not so sure that he had the strength to tell her about Kattie right now. What if she didn't understand why he had acted so impulsively, so irresponsibly? What if she agreed with him that he had been a jerk and told him to get lost?

God! But he had to tell her. Fighting his desire just to kiss her until they were both senseless, he gently disengaged Laura's arms from around his neck.

"Laura, about last night . . ." he began, eyes lowered, voice hoarse.

Oh, no, Laura thought, *here it comes. He's saying good-bye, he's going to leave me again.* She wanted to scream, to yell, to shout at him not to go. But the only thing that came out of her closed throat was a silly little squeak.

Michael's head snapped up at the tiny sound of pain Laura uttered. He forgot his speech and almost cried out himself when he saw the hint of tears clouding her beautiful eyes. His hand automatically went out to touch her soft cheek and he couldn't help caressing the rest of her delicate features.

With her hair wild and her makeup gone, she appeared

so young, so vulnerable, that he longed to hold her and rock her like a sick child.

Sick child! Michael had completely forgotten that there wasn't time for him to carefully explain to Laura right now. She had to get to the airport and back to her daughter.

"Laura, I was about to say that last night was incredible and there's nothing I'd like better than to just stay right here with you for the next year or two. But we have to get going, sweetheart. I know you haven't forgotten about that nine o'clock plane. And I certainly wouldn't want to be the cause of your missing it."

He pushed away abruptly so she wouldn't feel the hard evidence that belied his words.

"Oh, my God, I forgot all about Mai," Laura whispered to herself, guilt and desire and the tiniest hint of fear warring in her brain.

Miguel bounced off the bed and said a bit too cheerfully, "Why don't you just hop into the shower first, while I order us some breakfast from room service?"

Not quite understanding the false heartiness in his voice, Laura felt an abrupt wave of apprehension wash over her. Something was not right here. Yet, unable to put her nebulous suspicions into words, she could do nothing, except nod her acceptance of Miguel's suggestion and swing her legs over the edge of the bed.

Seeing him watch her with hooded eyes, Laura wrapped the top sheet around herself, strangely needing to cover her nakedness. She retrieved the small suitcase that held her toiletries and clean underwear. Then, quickly grabbing an outfit hanging in the closet, she bolted for the adjacent bathroom.

Locking the door behind her, she leaned her head back against the smoothly painted surface. Her confusion abruptly cleared and Laura's mind finally figured out why Miguel had literally plucked himself from her arms this morning.

You dummy, she mocked herself. *He's just answered the question you asked when you woke up: would a confirmed bachelor want any permanent place in your life? No, he would not!*

"Doesn't want me to miss my plane," she muttered. "Ha! Last night was incredible. Yeah! What he really meant to say was, 'Glad to have seen you, Laura. Thanks for spending the night with me, have to do it again in another fifteen years, or so. And by the way, why don't I order you a croissant and coffee to show my appreciation?' "

Wrenching the handles on the shower to full power, Laura stood under the hot, pulsing cascade, letting the spray wash away every trace of Michael's passion from her body . . . and the salty residue of her dreams from her face.

In the other room, Michael had just finished ordering a simple breakfast, emphasizing to room service that he had to get to the airport. As he lowered the telephone receiver, he realized that he was smiling. In fact, he knew he was grinning like a perfect idiot. But he felt so damned happy, so lucky to be alive on this most wonderful day in the history of the world!

Come on, hombre, get serious, he tried to caution himself. *There are still a few important barriers you have to cross before Laura can be yours.*

In spite of those unresolved problems, Michael just stood there, naked as a newborn babe, grinning. It was only when the shower stopped in the bathroom that he began looking for his scattered clothing.

Finding his shirt, he picked it up and absently started to dress, while his mind sorted out his next moves. After a quick breakfast, he would drive Laura to the airport. On the way, there'd be time enough to talk to her about Kattie.

He had just zipped his pants when in the same second the phone rang, someone knocked on the door, and Laura emerged from the bathroom.

Michael threw her a smile, grabbed the receiver, and reached over to open the door for their breakfast cart before the expression on Laura's face registered in his brain.

In the middle of trying to pay the waiter and greeting the person on the phone, Michael's eyes kept darting back to Laura, who stood glaring at him with cold, angry eyes.

The waiter finally backed out of the room, thanking Michael profusely, in a voice enriched by a heavy Spanish accent, for the generous tip.

"*No hay de que*," Michael automatically responded in the tongue and, as the door clicked shut, he finally realized that the feminine voice on the phone wasn't speaking in English.

"*Quién es? Con quién quiere hablar?*" he asked her, before he recognized a few German words. "Oh, excuse me, Marthe, I'll get Laura for you."

The words were barely out of his mouth before she stormed over and grabbed the instrument out of his hand. As she put the phone to her ear, Michael saw her glance at the light breakfast he had ordered, her eyes going from the basket full of flaky croissants, to the large carafe of steaming coffee the waiter had delivered.

Laura rewarded his thoughtfulness with such a vitriolic sneer of displeasure that he was surprised when his skin didn't start to peel.

What in the hell had gotten into her, Michael wondered. Why had she suddenly changed from the sweetly passionate lover of last night into this aloof icicle?

Michael felt his confusion turn to an anger of his own. But even as a hotly worded response formed in his brain, he listened to Laura speak to her housekeeper in rapid German. As he watched, every bit of color departed from her face.

Any thought of his own anger fled when he saw her fingers tighten on the phone until her knuckles turned white, and he knew that something must have happened to her daughter.

Michael quickly moved to Laura's side as she cradled the receiver. She stood with her hand on the phone, her eyes squeezed shut.

"Honey, sweetheart, what's the matter?" he asked, placing his hands on her shoulders.

Her eyes opened, but Laura didn't answer for long seconds, her gaze seemed to be focused some place on the other side of hell. Then she looked directly at Michael and finally answered his frantic question.

"She's gone, Miguel," Laura whispered. "Mai is gone."

EIGHT

"Gone? What do you mean gone," Michael demanded, holding her more tightly when it seemed that Laura's knees were about to buckle.

"She's run away. Marthe just found a note on Mai's pillow saying that she was going to take a bus to San Francisco. Oh, Miguel, she's only eleven. It's not safe for a little girl to travel alone. There're all sorts of parasites just waiting to get young runaways into their slimy hands."

"Now, just calm down, Laura. Your imagination is getting the better of you. Get packed while I telephone the bus terminal and ask them to watch out for your daughter. Do you know when she left?"

"Not exactly, it could have been any time after ten. It's an eight-hour drive by car, but I don't know how long the bus takes. Oh, just have them check the station, and the next bus arriving from Los Angeles," Laura directed, pulling her suitcase out of the closet and ramming her clothing into it.

Michael stood looking at her, longing to pull her into his arms and soothe away the panic-induced adrenaline that was making her movements so jerky and uncoordinated.

Instead, he turned toward the phone. His hand hovered

over the receiver when he had a sudden thought. "Laura, give me one of those pictures of Mai you told me about last night, so I can tell them what she looks like."

Laura immediately opened her purse and extracted her wallet. She slipped the latest photo of Mai out of the plastic covering and handed it to Miguel. Watching him examine her daughter's likeness, she remembered an important fact.

"Ah, Miguel, that picture was taken at the beginning of the school year, last September. Mai has . . . ah, changed a lot since then."

Michael looked up from the photo of the dainty-looking blond child. "Well, the basics—hair and eye color—must still be the same."

"Ah, not exactly," Laura muttered, knowing that she had to tell him.

"I don't understand, what . . ."

The harsh ring of the phone interrupted his confusion. Laura grabbed the receiver. "Yes, this is she speaking. Yes. Oh, thank God! I'll be right down to get her. At the main terminal? OK. I'll ask for you, Mr. Sanchez. Yes, in the dispatcher's office. Mr. Sanchez, please don't let her out of your sight. OK, all right, and thank you very much."

Laura cradled the receiver and then moved slowly to the bed, sinking down next to her half-packed suitcase.

"Mai's all right?" Michael queried, sitting next to her.

"Yes, at the bus terminal. She had enough sense to ask the bus driver to get her a cab to the Sir Francis Drake. He wisely took her to Mr. Sanchez, the dispatcher, and he immediately contacted me."

Laura suddenly leapt up. "Let me just call Marthe and tell her that Mai's safe. Then I'll have the desk cancel my plane reservation and get my bill ready. Taxis usually cruise around outside, right?"

"Yeah, but I have my car here. I'll get it out of the

parking garage and meet you in front of the building,'' he said, getting up from the bed.

"Oh, no need for you to do that, Miguel," Laura said forcefully, not forgetting his rush to be rid of her this morning.

"Look, Laura, there's no way I'm going to let you go to that terminal alone. I have some things that need to be said to you and I'm going to say them. Now, make your calls, finish packing, and get a bellboy to take down your luggage. I'll meet you out front in fifteen minutes. And be sure to eat one of those before you leave this room."

He pointed at the basket of croissants. Glaring at her, he grabbed one for himself and then slammed out the door.

"I'd rather starve, mister," Laura muttered, marching back to the phone. She'd also find a way to elude him downstairs and get to the bus terminal on her own.

Ten minutes later, Laura took a last look around for anything she might have forgotten. When her eyes strayed to the container of rolls, she muttered a mild curse and stomped over to the table. Wrapping two croissants in paper napkins, she jammed them into her purse, telling herself that Mai would probably be hungry.

In the lobby, Laura had just given the signed Visa slip to the desk clerk when the hairs on the back of her neck began to rise. Turning slightly, her head then snapped up several inches to find determined green eyes glittering at her.

"W–what are you doing here? I thought you'd be outside . . .''

"Just making sure everything's in order, that there were no last minute glitches that you needed help with," Michael stated blandly. Reading the guilt on Laura's face, he knew he had been right. He could see that she had planned to ditch him.

Without another word, Michael just bent down to pick up her luggage. He tucked the smaller suitcase under his arm and then grabbed the big one. Taking Laura's elbow with his free hand, he led her stiff little body out to his waiting car.

After he slipped the doorman a bill in return for watching the vehicle, Michael quickly placed Laura into the passenger seat and then stowed her luggage in the trunk.

As it turned out, Michael never got to talk to Laura on the way to the bus station. For one thing, the terminal was only a few blocks from the hotel. And for another, he could see that she felt so uptight, so worried about her daughter that she could barely sit still on her seat.

And there was no way Michael could say everything he had to say—in just the right way—in a ten-minute drive. No, he'd have to postpone his explanation yet again.

Nearing the terminal, he spotted a free parking space not a block away. Pulling into the opening, he cut the engine and turned to speak to Laura. But she'd already released her seatbelt and bolted out the door.

After shoving a quarter in the parking meter, Michael sprinted to catch up with Laura, reaching her just as she pushed into the station. He grabbed her arm and swung her around.

"Laura, if you don't calm down you're going to overreact in front of your daughter and blow it."

"Blow it? OK, since you're such an expert, you tell me what I should do," she all but shouted.

"No, I'm not an expert, but I have been around enough children to know that Mai has got to be scared to death. She's defied you and probably thinks that you hate her."

All the antagonism Laura felt seeped away in the heavy sigh she exhaled. "Lord, you're right, Miguel. We've been at sixes and sevens a lot lately, and I've heard that accusation from Mai more than once in the past few months."

"Well, don't worry, it goes with the age group. So,

just take a deep breath and when you see her give her a big hug and not a lecture."

"That may be easier said than done," Laura said with a wry smile, "but I'll give it my best shot."

After asking a passing employee where the dispatcher's office was, Laura and Michael walked to the door the woman indicated. Taking the deep breath he had prescribed, Laura knocked and went in. Michael followed a step behind her.

He looked around the room and didn't see anyone except the dark-haired man seated at a computer terminal. When Laura approached him, the uniformed official looked up, smiled a silent greeting, and then called over his shoulder.

"Mai, honey, I think your mom and dad are here."

The man had made a natural mistake, but Michael couldn't help feeling a warm wave of pleasure at being identified as Laura's husband. He threw her a quick glance, wanting to see if she had reacted in the same way. But her attention was centered on the small, slight figure who had just risen from a chair, half hidden by a tall file cabinet.

Michael felt his mouth fall open, but he managed to repress a shout of laughter at the sight of the young girl. It became clear why Laura had been so vague about her daughter's current description. In place of the long, blond hair he had seen in her school photo, Mai now sported an asymmetrical cut. Shoulder length on one side, the other half of her head had been close-cropped and featured several shaved bands, while six-inch spikes radiated around her crown.

Her clothing was equally strange. Mai wore an outfit Madonna might have designed. All in black—from calf-high leather boots to a miniskirt and leather jacket. She also had on a corset-like bustier that she would not fill for several years.

All together, Mai's get-up epitomized a parent's worst

nightmare, but Michael's impulse to laugh died at the sound of the little girl's high-pitched, exhausted wail.

"Mom? Oh, Mommy, I'm so glad you're here."

Laura had felt a brief surge of dismay at the clothing that adorned her daughter's slight body. Where? When? How had Mai ever come to own such a bizarre collection, she wondered. But, instead of questioning her, Laura just held out her arms and enfolded Mai's hot little form.

Even through the multi-layering of her clothing, heat radiated from her. A heat so unnatural that Laura pulled back and placed a hand on her daughter's forehead.

"My God, you are burning up. I bet your temperature is a hundred and two, if it's a degree," she whispered.

"I feel awful," Mai confirmed. "My throat hurts when I swallow and my left ear is aching like crazy."

"And you've been traveling in a drafty bus all night. Mai, how could you have done such a foolish thing?" Laura began, completely forgetting the good advice Miguel had given her, and her own fine intentions.

Mai reacted instantly to the change in her mother's voice. Pulling out of her arms, she backed away, reaching down to gather a large, well-worn leather case to her slight chest.

For the first time, Laura noticed that besides a backpack, her daughter had brought along the Guarnari, her grandmother's violin. Knowing how much Mai treasured the instrument, and how well she always took care of it, Laura felt her anger drain away. Bringing it along meant that Mai was seriously troubled. More troubled than Laura had thought.

"Honey, I'm sorry. I'm not really mad at you. I'm just worried that your cold has turned into something far more serious."

"Yeah, I know how worried you are about me. That's why you're never home anymore. All you're really worried about is making money." Mai began to sob, but even as the first tears reached her cheeks, she put a hand over her ear and looked up at the fluorescent fixture in the middle of the ceiling. "It hurts, that light hurts my ears," she wailed.

Hearing the real pain in the child's voice, Michael turned to the dispatcher, whose face showed his concern for the little girl.

"Mr. Sanchez, can I use your phone? I'm going to call my doctor and ask him to see the child right away."

"Miguel, thank you, but that's not necessary," Laura said, putting an arm around her daughter. "We're covered by a state-wide HMO, and I'm sure they have a clinic or hospital nearby. Right, Mr. Sanchez?" She named the organization.

"Only a few blocks from here," he confirmed. "But you don't want to go there. That place is a zoo, believe me."

Laura just looked at the man in dismay, while Mai tugged insistently on her hand.

"Mom, Mom, who is this guy with you?" she asked, looking at Michael. When her mother stood mutely for long seconds, Mai asked him directly. "Are you a business associate of my mother's?"

"No, an old friend, I'm Michael O'Brian . . ." he began, holding out his hand.

"This is Miguel O'Brian," Laura said belatedly, finally getting her tongue into gear.

Mai looked between the two of them for a second, speculation alive in her intelligent little face.

"We were in the Peace Corps together fifteen years ago, and we met by accident at the hotel," Laura elaborated, seeing the wheels turning behind those precociously wise eyes.

Mai's interest in Miguel vanished, as she clutched her ear again and moaned in pain.

Before Laura could do more than put a comforting arm around her daughter, Miguel again queried Mr. Sanchez about the use of his phone. The dispatcher quickly gave his permission.

Within five minutes, Michael had made arrangements with his doctor to see Mai in his office. Then, thanking Mr. Sanchez for his help, he escorted mother and daughter out of the terminal.

"Oh, oh. You better wait inside the door while I get the car," Michael advised, when he noticed the early morning breeze whipping bits of paper and dust around them.

"Thank you," Laura murmured at his thoughtfulness, and was rewarded with one of Miguel's potent smiles.

Back inside the terminal, Laura stood with Mai, both of them watching Miguel's long-legged stride eat up the sidewalk. When he disappeared from view, Mai looked up at her mother and grinned, her pain obviously under control for the moment.

"That guy's something else, Mom. A real gentleman. And obviously crazy about you. Play your cards right and he'll pop the question before we leave for home. If he makes a decent salary, I think you should accept."

Laura frowned sternly, but then couldn't hold on to the slightly hysterical laughter that bubbled out of her lips. By now, she should have been used to the adult-sounding pronouncements that came from her eleven-year-old's mouth. Yet, half the time she got caught by surprise when Mai's analytical mind made instant sense out of the most complex problems.

"I'm afraid that this time you don't have all the facts, darling," Laura told her daughter. "Miguel O'Brian may be something else, but he is not interested in marrying me, and I'm not going to marry him . . . no matter how much money he makes."

"We'll see," the girl said in reply. Just then the long, black Mercedes pulled up in front. Mai took one look at Miguel's car and muttered, "Good, he's loaded."

Laura stifled a groan, watching Miguel come around the vehicle and start toward them. He opened the terminal door, ushering them outside. When Mai stumbled on the threshold, he swept the child into his arms, carrying her the rest of the way to the car.

He placed her in the backseat and then tried to relieve her of the violin case.

"No, you can't have it," she protested.

"I'll just put in it the trunk, so you can stretch out on the seat if you want to," he explained.

"You don't understand. This was my grandmother's legacy to me, but it really belongs to the world. I'm lucky to have the use of it for my lifetime, so it's my responsibility to keep it safe."

Laura smiled to herself, watching Miguel do a doubletake at Mai's mature phraseology. "She'll feel better if she has it. It really is a special instrument." *Worth more than everything else the Eastens owned*, she silently reminded herself, *and one hell of a problem to keep insured.*

Michael just shook his head and got into the driver's seat. Laura had told him how smart her daughter was, but this child was awesome. Starting the car, he drove slowly through the city streets until reaching the freeway leading to the Bay Bridge.

When Laura saw the sign indicating that they were going toward Berkeley and Oakland, her head snapped around to look at Miguel's strongly cut profile.

"Just where *is* this doctor of yours located?" she asked.

"A few miles from my house," he replied.

"And your house is across this bridge?"

"I live about ten miles northeast of Walnut Creek," he said, pointing to one of the other destinations on the sign.

That didn't help Laura much.

"Miguel, just tell me how long this trip is going to take."

"Barring any tie-ups through the Caldecott tunnel bores, about thirty minutes to Walnut Creek. At this time of day, it's only fifteen minutes further to Clayton, where I live."

"I should have gone to the HMO like I wanted to," Laura muttered.

"Mr. O'Brian, Mr. O'Brian," Mai interrupted from the back seat. "That sign said we're on the Bay Bridge. This is the one that fell during the earthquake, isn't it? And even though it happened at rush hour, only one or two people got killed, right?"

"I think so. But don't worry, Mai, just a small section on the upper deck fell. That's been fixed and the rest of the bridge has been safety inspected," Michael answered. "And how about calling me Mike, like Kattie's kids do."

"Kattie's kids?" Laura asked immediately, the wealth of affection in his voice triggering something very much like a red light in her brain.

"Ah . . . ah . . . my neighbor's children," he said, sending Laura a guilty glance.

"So, where is the section that fell?" Mai asked, leaning as far forward as her seatbelt would allow.

"I'm not really sure. Maybe if you look overhead, you'll see the newer metal."

"No. No, I don't see anything," she said after a minute of intense examination. "Gee, this isn't like being on other bridges. I can hardly see the water."

"Yeah, the trip into San Francisco on the top deck is a lot more scenic, but look through the supports to your left. That's the Golden Gate Bridge over in the distance. And we're just coming up on Treasure Island, where there's a big naval base."

Once off the bridge, Michael negotiated the maze of crisscrossing highways, taking the high, curving ramp that led away from Oakland and Berkeley toward Walnut Creek.

"If you watch between those buildings on your left, Mai, you might be able to see a clear space where the Cypress Structure used to be. That's where . . ."

"Oh, God, Miguel, don't encourage her," Laura hissed, but Mai's excited voice cut over hers.

"Oh, I know all about the Cypress Structure. During the earthquake that's where the whole top part fell and squashed all those cars flat. I saw everything on television. They got a bunch of people out of there alive, even days later."

"Mai, darling, you're looking flushed. Why don't you try lying back and closing your eyes," Laura suggested, after giving Miguel a telling look that indicated just what she thought he should do with any more gruesome tourist information.

Somehow, knowing the source of her anger this time, her righteous glare only amused him. Michael had to fight to keep his mouth straight, so he tried not to meet Laura's eyes again. But at the sudden silence in the car, he couldn't help glancing in the rearview mirror.

Amazingly, Mai had taken her mother's advice and actually closed her eyes. Her slightly congested breathing evened out, and he knew that she would be deeply asleep before they got to the Caldecott Tunnel. Which was probably a good thing, Michael thought, just before the car slid into the half-mile-long bore that cut through the hills of Berkeley. The stark remains of a wildfire that had killed twenty-five and burned thousands of homes were still very evident on both sides of the tunnel.

He finally chanced casting an eye at Laura when they exited the tunnel and rolled back into the bright morning sunshine. He saw her long eyelashes flicker, but she wouldn't look his way, stubbornly keeping her head turned toward the window and the passing devastation.

He also noticed Laura gnaw at her lower lip and clench her hands on her purse. Michael would bet a mint that she wasn't seeing the burned hills through which the highway wound.

Laura obviously had a real problem with her daughter. Michael felt tempted to question her about Mai's exotic appearance and the morbid interest in disasters she seemed to have. Yet, he was afraid that anything he said would deepen the seething anger he sensed in her. He didn't know what he had done to merit this treatment.

Well, of course, he knew that he *had* done something awful to her, but Laura didn't know about it . . . yet. There was absolutely no way she could have found out about Kattie.

As they passed Lafayette, Michael jockeyed to the right, out of the fast lane, to take the Ygnacio Valley Road exit. At ten-thirty in the morning, the traffic flowed smoothly and they quickly passed through the small city of Walnut Creek.

Ygnacio continued its path northward, passing through ancient sand dunes that now were covered with browned grass and grazing cattle. Reaching a straight stretch of roadway, Michael abruptly decided that he had had enough of the silent treatment. Pulling well off the asphalt, he stopped the car and set the brake.

Turning to Laura, he kept his voice low and controlled, so he wouldn't wake her daughter. "All right, spit it out. What in the hell is going on?"

"Nothing for you to worry about," Laura protested. "Mai is just going through a phase. She's trying to assert her personality with that haircut and the clothes. Although I'll admit I never saw this particular getup before."

"I'm not asking about Mai," Michael said with slow deliberation. "But now that you've brought it up, don't you think that there's something more serious here than just a passing phase. I mean, plenty of kids wear freaky stuff at her age, but the business on the bridge and near the Cypress Structure is really weird. It sounds as if she collects disasters!"

"You were the one who pointed out the freeway that collapsed. But you're wrong, she doesn't collect disasters. She collects disaster *survivors*. And she only started doing that when I began lecturing around the country, taking a dozen plane flights every month. She's trying to reassure herself that even when there's an accident, or disaster, that *some* people can survive." The defiance suddenly drained out of Laura's voice. "Oh, Miguel, what have I done to her?"

Biting off a harsh curse at his insensitivity, Michael unsnapped his seatbelt and slid over to gather Laura in his arms. Her body shook with suppressed grief, obviously struggling to hold in her sobs so Mai didn't awaken.

"Shh, shh, sweetheart," he crooned, trying to ease away the shuddering in her body by caressing her nape and then running his hand down her back.

Michael tried to ignore the heat rising in his body, as Laura slowly quieted and tightened her grip around his waist. This is just to comfort *her*, he kept telling himself, when she relaxed against him. But he was well aware that the firm flesh of her breasts pressed against him, and that somehow his knee had separated hers, and his thigh fit in the snug trap made by the stretched material of her straight skirt.

"Don't cry, Laura, I wasn't saying that you're a bad mother. And now that you know what the problem is, I'm sure you'll do what's necessary."

Laura's head snapped up from its cushion on Miguel's broad shoulder. "Necessary, what do you mean, necessary?"

"You'll quit traveling."

"Quit? How can I quit? I've got too many expenses to quit."

"I don't understand. Surely your husband had insurance. And what about your father? I know you told me last night that he isn't wealthy, but if things are tight, can't he help? Not that it matters anymore, I'll be . . ."

Michael bit off his sentence. He couldn't say that he'd be seeing to all of her needs from now on. He didn't have that right yet.

Laura shook her head. "My father is retired. He doesn't have any money to spare. As for Jerry, of course he carried insurance. We both did. His policy covered hundreds of thousands of dollars toward his medical expenses, and mine took care of even more. But do you have any idea what's involved in repeated hospitalizations these days? After the insurance ran out, the savings went, the condominum went, and even the car. Jerry just couldn't bring himself to ask for state assistance, and I wholeheartedly agreed with him. So, when he died, I vowed to pay off his debts in full. That's why I quit classroom teaching and became a lecturer.

"The company pays me three times what I could earn in a regular teaching situation. If I stay with them, I'll be free and clear within a few years. Mai understands that our family honor is involved, and she agrees that we have to pay everything back. At least, she agrees consciously. We'll just have to work on making her subconscious behave, too."

Michael didn't know what to say. Here, he had been thinking that even though Laura had lost her husband, her life had been relatively problem free. Instead, she had suffered both emotional and financial traumas that would have crushed many women. Yet, she had faced her problems with strength and dignity.

He allowed himself the luxury of dropping a quick kiss on her forehead. "I'm sorry, Laura. I just didn't understand. You have my permission to give me a swift kick as soon as we get done at the doctor's office."

As Miguel moved back into the driver's seat, Laura wanted to cry out, to protest the loss of his warmth, his strength. For a few seconds in his arms, all of her problems had seemed very solvable.

When he started the engine and pulled back onto the road, the total reality of her situation came back in full force. Miguel was a kind man, a marvelous lover, but he obviously didn't want to get involved with her on any long-term basis. So after today, she would do what she had done for years. She would handle her problems, her worries, and her loneliness all by herself.

* * *

Five minutes later, Michael pulled into a small medical office suite located on the corner of an otherwise residential street. He stopped the car and shepherded mother and daughter into Dave Green's office.

Laura looked around the waiting room, noting the cartoon animals stenciled on the walls and the very small chairs that were intermixed with normal-sized seats.

"You go to a pediatrician?" she challenged Miguel.

"Of course not," he laughed. "Dave's a good friend and I thought that he'd be the best one for Mai to see." Michael walked to the inner door and knocked sharply. A few seconds later, it was opened by a short, redheaded man wearing a sports shirt and walking shorts.

"Gee, Dave, did I catch you on your way to a golf game?" Michael asked ruefully, indicating his outfit.

"Naw, I had finished already and just came by to check some files before I went home. The only way Cindy lets me get in a weekend round is if I tee off at the crack of dawn. Well, come in, come in." He gestured to Mai and Laura, not even batting an eye at the girl's hair or attire. "Why don't you introduce me, Mike?"

"Oh, I'm sorry. Dave. This is Mai Easten, and her mother, Laura. Laura's an old friend from Peace Corps days. It seems that Mai has a sore throat and an earache."

"OK, Mai. Let's go into an examining room and see what's what. Mike, why don't you check out the latest *Humpty Dumpty* magazine, while I see to this young lady?"

Michael felt himself turning red. He hadn't thought about Dave listening to Mai's heart and lungs, and that she would have to remove her clothing for the stethoscope.

"Yeah, sure, I'll just wait out here."

He had almost resorted to thumbing through the children's magazine when the trio finally exited from the examining room.

Laura had her arm around Mai, and looked worried as

she conversed with Dave. "Well, Doctor, if you say flying is dangerous for Mai with her ear infection, of course we won't go home that way. Perhaps we can catch the Amtrak and take a taxi home from the station in L.A."

"No, with that fever and a possible strep infection, I don't recommend that Mai travel at all. I'm sending the swab I took to the lab for culturing. I'd really like to get another look at her in a couple days, say Monday, to see how the antibiotic I prescribed is working. Of course, you are free to get another opinion."

"Oh, Dr. Green, I don't need a second opinion. I'm very grateful that you could see us on such short notice. We'll find a motel nearby and come back on Monday," she confirmed.

"I think that's for the best. I'll leave a note for my office manager to work you in during the morning. Just give her a call after nine. Is your throat feeling less sore now, Mai?"

"It sure is. That stuff you sprayed really helped."

"Good, it'll last until your mom can fill the prescriptions. Just take the antibiotics and painkillers on schedule, and that sore throat and ear will be history before you know it. And even though you feel better now, be sure to get plenty of rest. No dancing till dawn," he admonished, looking at her outfit.

"Darn, guess I'll have to break my date with Tom Cruise," Mai smiled, and Laura felt a wonderful sense of relief that her daughter sounded like her old self . . . the cheerful child she hadn't seen in several months.

"Thanks for everything, Dave," Michael said.

"No problem, I owe you one for all the patients you keep steering my way. Say hello to Kattie and her kids for me," the pediatrician said, walking them to the outer door.

Michael knew that his face had turned red once again, but he just tossed off a farewell wave and led the way to the car.

"Kattie and the kids are the neighbors you mentioned before?" Laura asked trying to sound casual as she recalled the other reference to the woman's children he had made while they were driving over the Bay Bridge. This Kattie person seemed to crop up in a whole lot of converaations this morning.

"They're my next-door neighbors," Michael said. "I'll tell you all about . . . them, right after we get this young lady settled."

He gave Mai's shoulder an affectionate squeeze before opening the passenger doors. Then, remembering her concern about her violin, he quickly retrieved the case they had stored in the trunk and placed it on the backseat next to Mai.

Halfway into her own seat, Laura stopped and looked around the street, again noticing all the houses. "Miguel, speaking of getting Mai settled, is there a motel near here that's also close to a drugstore? I want to put her right to bed, and then get these prescriptions."

"Don't worry, Laura, I'll drive you to a pharmacy a couple of blocks from here, and then you'll come stay with me at my home."

"Your home? Oh, I don't want to put you to any trouble . . ."

"Hey, that's a great idea, Mike," Mai piped up. "I'll bet you have a neat house."

Mai's enthusiasm overrode her mother's soft objection, but Michael said firmly to Laura, "It's no trouble. I have people stay all the time, business associates and the like. That's why I've got guest rooms."

It wasn't the only reason, but he didn't want to think again about his family's refusal to visit him. Instead, he glared fiercely at Laura, almost trying to will her to accept when it appeared that she was going to protest again.

His suggestion had been off the top of his head, but the more he thought about it, the more sense it made. Mai would rest better in his home than at a noisy motel. And with Kattie in Arkansas and Jeff not due back until tomorrow, Michael could have the time he needed to finally come clean with Laura. Besides, he was terrified that if he let her out of his sight, she would somehow slip away from him—forever.

"Thank you, Miguel, I really appreciate this," Laura reluctantly agreed, her maternal concern winning over stubborn pride. *So what if he didn't feel the same way she did? So what if last night had meant so little to him? So what!*

She had Mai's well-being to think of. All Laura had to do was stay out of Miguel's way. Why torture herself with "what-might-have-been" dreams?

"I promise that we won't be any bother," she firmly told him.

Now, that is a laugh, Michael thought. *Just sitting next to her on this car seat bothers me.*

The way her blouse and skirt clung lovingly to her body made him remember the firm, silken skin he had stroked in the night. The perfume of her own unique fragrance caused him to take deep breaths, just to capture more of her scent. The tendrils of soft blond hair that had escaped from her controlling chignon, tempted him to slowly take out each and every pin, so he could bury his face in the thick-falling mass.

No bother? Hell, he thought, savagely twisting the key in the ignition, *I've never been so hot and bothered in my life!* And worst of all, he could do absolutely nothing about it. He couldn't even touch Laura, not until Kattie came back from Arkansas and he asked to be released from their engagement.

NINE

After getting Mai her medicine, along with a soft drink to take the first dose, Michael pulled out onto Clayton Road. Following the curving boulevard east, the car soon left new housing tracts and commercial businesses behind. As the streets grew further apart and the homes became larger, weathered redwood property fences took on the added responsibility of corralling fine-looking riding horses.

Several miles later, Michael turned off the main road onto a winding macadam street that spiraled up to the lower flanks of four-thousand-foot Mt. Diablo. The mountain always seemed far higher to him than it really was because Clayton was not much above sea level. Finally pulling into his gravel-covered driveway, Michael stopped in front of his three-car garage.

Laura's view of the rest of his house was obstructed by the garage and the heavy vegetation that flanked it. He activated the electronic device attached to his windshield visor and the segmented door rolled up, revealing a Jeep and an orderly array of gardening and carpentry tools inside.

"I'll get your luggage and Mai's violin in a minute," he said to her, after pulling the Mercedes into its slot.

"Let's go through the front entrance. There's something I want to show Mai on the way."

Holding Mai's hand, Laura followed behind Miguel, keeping her eyes on the uneven flagstone path that wrapped around the right side of the garage. She almost ran into his broad back when he abruptly stopped. He grabbed her shoulders, both to stabilize her and to turn her toward the north.

"Now, both of you look toward the horizon," Miguel urged mother and daughter. "Can you see the glint of water over there, Mai?"

The view was literally breathtaking. A sigh caught in Laura's throat, and she heard Mai give a small gasp of appreciation, too. Beneath their feet, the property fell away slowly to reveal a terraced embankment that was covered by a bright froth of flowering bushes and an extensive variety of dwarf fruit trees.

Laura quickly picked out apple and pear, several kinds of citrus, and the shiny red flowers that would soon produce a luscious crop of pomegranates. But even as her eyes took in the bounty, her attention danced away—beyond the eclectic array of large homes studding the lower hills—to the ancient sand dunes that rolled endlessly toward the horizon and stopped only when they encountered a wide expanse of sparkling water.

"Is that the Pacific?" Mai asked.

"No, we're thirty-five miles east of the ocean proper," Michael explained. "You're looking at Suisun Bay, which is part of the Sacramento River. It's an estuary and the water eventually flows into San Francisco Bay and the sea. Suisun Bay is what I wanted to point out to you, Mai. Do you remember hearing about a whale that left the ocean and went swimming up a river a few years ago?"

Mai nodded her head. "Humphrey, the Humpbacked Whale."

"Right! Well, he entered San Francisco Bay under the Golden Gate Bridge we saw this morning and came all the way up here, and then swam eastward into the Delta region where the water gets pretty shallow."

"Yeah, and all those boats and people spent days turning him around and guiding him back into the ocean. But he keeps returning and causing all sorts of trouble. One time he beached himself on a sandbar and they had to dig him out. Remember, Mom, I told you that either he was very smart and too curious for his own good, or . . ."

"Or that he was the dunce of his pod, and a disgrace to whale intelligence in general," Michael finished for her. "My own thoughts exactly."

While the two of them shared a laugh over their identical assessment of Humphrey's brain power, Laura watched Miguel run an affectionate hand through the longer hair on the right side of Mai's head. Her daughter looked up at him, with something very like adoration in her eyes.

Which was completely unlike the girl. Laura squeezed her own eyes shut for an instant. Mai had always been slow to warm up to new people. Even as a baby, even before Laura had warned her daughter about not talking to strangers. Beyond the normal fears any mother had for her child, Laura also had found it necessary to stress to Mai that she could never talk to anyone about her grandfather, or reveal anything about Gustav Nordheim's condition.

In the past, Mai had always heeded her mother's advice, learning to make very sure of acquaintances before opening up to them. Yet, just two hours after meeting Miguel O'Brian, Mai was chatting away with him like he was her very best friend. It was clear that Miguel really did know how to relate to kids.

At the thought, Laura opened her eyes again and searched the path to her left, trying to locate the neighbor's house he had mentioned. But nothing was visible through the thick vegetation in that direction. Twisting to look behind her, Laura found that she was facing the main part of Miguel's house. And it had to be the most beautiful home she had ever seen.

The split-level structure had been built right into the side of the mountain, appearing to be carved from the living rock. The weathered stucco finish was the same color as the native sandstone. Even this close, Laura found that she had to focus hard to see where the house left off and the mountain began.

"How marvelous," she whispered in the tiniest of voices.

But somehow, Miguel heard her quiet exclamation and he turned to look at her. Laura could only smile and point to the structure. "Your home is magnificent," she finally managed.

"Mom, Mom, it's just like the Pueblo Indian houses we saw in New Mexico."

"New Mexico?" Michael asked dumbly, very aware of the tingling sensation that began to run up and down his spine. The *Kachinas* were back again, warning that they were about to brew up more mischief for him. Forcefully pushing the feeling away, he tried to concentrate on what Mai was saying.

"Yeah, we went to Albuquerque three years ago, on our way to California," she revealed. "All our furniture and stuff was traveling cross-country on the moving van, so Mom decided that we'd stop and see all the interesting places, instead of just flying nonstop.

"We toured Mammoth Cave in Kentucky, and the Alamo in Texas, and before we visited my grandfather in the . . . in his place in Arizona, we went to Albuquerque. We took a tour and saw the Petroglyph National Monument and . . ."

"You're from Albuquerque, Miguel, aren't you?" Laura interrupted her daughter, trying to stop Mai's uncharacteristic babbling.

"I went to school there, but I was born farther north," he explained, before thinking about what he was saying.

"Santa Fe?"

"No, Taos." Michael said shortly, fighting to control his strangely wayward tongue. He tried never to think about Taos. "Say, Mai, we're forgetting that you're a sick little *muchacha*. Come on and let's get you inside. Maybe when you're feeling better, we'll have time to walk one of the trails up there on Mt. Diablo. Or, maybe your mom will let me teach you how to ride a horse. I have a couple of fine animals in the corral." He gestured to the path to his right.

"You do? You do!" Mai's fingers tugged on Michael's hand, her eyes glowed with anticipation. "Would you really teach me? I mean, I already know how to ride a little. Mom's an expert and can jump and make the horse do all sorts of tricks. It's just that we haven't had time to practice since we moved from Washington. Could Mike teach me more, Mom?" Mai looked beseechingly at her mother.

Forgetting to turn the key he had just inserted into his front door, Michael also stared at Laura. He never would have pictured that slight body and those slender, white hands controlling a half ton of horse flesh in a jump.

Laura's mouth quirked, reading Miguel's mind. "Steeplechase and dressage, sort of R and R. After handling biology classes with forty teenagers at a time, matching wits with a horse seemed like a vacation." Her smile faltered when she glanced again at Mai's expectant face.

"Mai, we're only going to be here until you're well enough to travel, so you won't have time to accept Miguel's kind offer. But I do promise you that we'll look into finding a stable and riding trails near us when we get back home."

"Oh, you'll never have time," Mai complained, the happy light in her eyes becoming a hot-blue challenge. "Even if you did, I'll bet Mike knows lots of things about horses that you don't."

Laura heard the nascent hero worship in Mai's voice. She had to put a stop to it right now. As she had just told her daughter, they would only be here a short time. She couldn't allow Miguel to work his way into her daughter's heart, and then leave Mai even more needy than before.

It was bad enough that he had rekindled Laura's feelings for him. But *she* was an adult. She was capable of surviving yet another loss without being paralyzed by the pain. Mai was just a child, a child who had already faced the death of her father, and the tragic knowledge that her brilliant grandfather lived in a nightmare world far worse than death.

So, in order to break her daughter's growing attachment to Miguel, Laura reached deeply into her own hurtful memories. "Mai, I'm sure that Miguel is very experienced with horses. But don't forget who taught me to ride . . . your father. And *he* was a champion. Remember the scrapbooks I've showed you, sweetheart? You haven't forgotten that your father made the Olympic team, have you?"

"Oh, Mom, I didn't forget. You know that I can't forget," she said, every bit of antagonism gone from her voice. "It's just that Dad never taught *me* how to ride."

"He wanted to, Mai, he really wanted to. But by the time you were old enough, he was too sick, and then . . ."

"And then he died," Mai finished for her, touching her mother's cheek with a gentle hand. She smiled with grave maturity. "Mom, I'd love to go riding with you in L.A. When we get back home, the first thing I'll do is look in the yellow pages and find us some horses to rent."

Laura hugged her daughter to her, so proud of her loving little heart. Then her eyes locked on Miguel's face. His expression was impossible to read, but Laura felt he had to be condemning her, which he had every right to do.

She had just manipulated Mai's emotions, cynically using her daughter's memories of Jerry to keep Mai from making Miguel into a father substitute.

Michael saw the tears shimmering in Laura's eyes, and he could have kicked himself. He knew most kids were crazy about horses, but he should have gotten Laura's permission before dangling that carrot in front of Mai.

It was just that he liked Mai and he wanted the girl to like him, too. Shamefully, he also knew he was hoping that Mai would be in his corner, if her mother decided that he was a complete jerk after he explained to her about Kattie.

He would need all the help he could get in a few minutes, when he finally told Laura about his less-than-honest behavior with her since last night.

Even though he felt as if his fears were marching in bold letters across his forehead, Michael couldn't tear his eyes away from Laura's. He just stared at her until Mai pulled out of her mother's arms and turned toward him.

"Mike, I'm really tired, and I think my ear is starting to hurt again. Could you show me where I'll be sleeping?"

Galvanized by the weak sound of Mai's voice, Michael rushed to open the front door. He quickly ushered them past the entryway and down the long hallway that led to the guest rooms.

Laura had just a glimpse of Miguel's living area before he whisked them along a corridor. She only had time for the fleeting impression that wood-planked floors had been covered with bright woven scatter rugs and that the high, far wall was made out of stone.

Then they were in the large, brightly decorated guest room, and Laura was helping Mai out of her jacket.

"I thought that you'd like to be together and this room has twin beds. The closet's over here," Miguel said, indicating one door. "And a private bathroom is over there."

"I'm for that," Mai said, heading for the latter.

Laura watched her daughter disappear into the bedroom's lavatory.

"If you'd rather have a room of your own . . ."

Startled by the concern in Miguel's voice, Laura hastened to reassure him. "No, no, this is just fine for us."

The light, airy curtains and matching flowered bedspreads seemed to have been chosen with a young girl in mind, and Mai would have sold her soul for that corner fireplace in her bedroom at home. The tone of the furnishings puzzled Laura, but she held back asking the obvious questions.

Instead she just said, "It's a lovely room, Miguel, and you're right, I prefer keeping a close eye on Mai."

Besides, this is so much safer than having a bedroom all to myself, she thought. Sleeping here, there would be no temptation for her to fight, no midnight urge to go seek out Miguel's bed and beg him to take her in his arms.

"Well, I'll just go get your luggage. Be back in a minute," he promised, slipping out of the room.

It was probably more like three minutes, but Laura had barely sat down on an inviting armchair and closed her eyes when he returned. Somehow, he had managed to pick up her suitcases and Mai's backpack in one hand, while carefully holding the violin case in the other.

"Here, let me help you with those," she said, stifling a huge yawn, while using her stockinged toes to search the plush carpet for her shoes.

"Hey, don't bother putting those back on." Miguel said, depositing his burden. "In fact, why don't you get undressed and take a nap along with Mai? Unless you'd rather have something to eat first. Maybe that would be better. You've just had a croissant all day, and . . . You did have a roll, didn't you?"

"Did anyone ever tell you that you'd make a good Jewish mother, Miguel?" Laura asked in turn, sidestepping his question. She was not about to tell him about the stale little package in her purse. When they found her at the bus station, Mai had been in no condition to eat anything and Laura had completely forgotten about the croissants.

"No, you're the first person to accuse me of that." He chuckled.

"Well, sleep sounds a lot more inviting than food right now," she said with an answering smile.

"Good, I'll wake you in a couple hours for a late lunch," Miguel offered. "Until then, I'll be making up some sleep on my own."

The oblique statement was the only reference he had made all day to the night they had spent together. But the slow, sweet smile he bestowed upon Laura held a wealth of remembrance and ripe satisfaction.

That grin made her catch her breath and tripped her heart into a curious little two-step. Looking into the place where she kept her most precious dreams, Laura saw a tiny spark of hope begin to glow.

Miguel seemed about to say something more when Mai poked her head around the bathroom door.

"Hey, Mom, there's soap and brand-new toothbrushes in here. But what am I going to do for a nightgown? I forgot to bring one."

"Oh, I think there's something here you can use." Miguel went to one of the two dressers that flanked the beds. Pulling open a drawer, he reached in and presented Mai with a huge T-shirt. When she held it up, Laura saw that it had a University of New Mexico emblem on the front and a store tag dangling from one sleeve.

"Fantastic, Mike, this is just fantastic," Mai said, molding the shirt to her body.

"Great, now everybody get some sleep. Lunch is at three," Miguel called, already on his way down out the door.

While Mai changed in the bathroom, Laura hesitated only a few seconds before she succumbed to temptation and pulled out the same drawer Miguel had opened. In it she found a bright selection of clothing that would thrill any teenaged girl. Sweaters, blouses, jeans—each and every garment brand new with the manufacturers' tags still in place.

Slowly pushing the drawer back into place, Laura stood

looking at the door Miguel had closed behind him. A dozen questions fought for dominance in her brain. She reluctantly put them aside when Mai came out of the bathroom and plopped down on one of the beds.

"OK, young lady, time to take this other medicine Dr. Green gave you. Says here that it'll make you a bit sleepy, but at least your throat won't feel scratchy and keep waking you up."

Mai bit into the liquid-filled lozenge without a word. After checking that Miguel had safely stowed her violin in a corner, she climbed under the covers and curled into her favorite sleeping position.

"Don't wake me for lunch, Mom. I think that I'll just sleep for a year or two," she announced, before closing her eyes and quickly drifting off.

Laura smiled at the angelic picture her daughter made, now that she had taken off that awful outfit and the shaved half of her head was hidden by the pillow.

In spite of all the worry and upheaval her arrival had caused this morning, Laura felt happy that Mai was here. It seemed as if much of the anger and rebellion her daughter had shown in the last few months had disappeared, somewhere on the bus ride to San Francisco. The sweet, thoughtful child that she had feared was gone forever had come back to her.

A rueful grin tugged at Laura's mouth. *That's a whole lot of wishful thinking on your part, lady,* she scolded herself. She had spent enough years dealing with adolescents to know this was just a lull in the storm of growing up. She and Mai would have to weather many a tempest in the future.

Yet, for the first time in months, Laura believed that there was hope for their relationship, even if calm sailing might be a decade away.

Sighing, she slipped out of her clothes and after letting down her hair, she pulled a nightshirt over her head. Closing her eyes when she lay back on the pillow, she willed her mind to shut off.

Several minutes later, it became evident that her brain was not cooperating. Scenes from the previous night were playing an encore behind her eyelids. She punched the pillow, adjusted the covers . . . and remembered. Uttering a low sound of disgust, Laura debated getting up and taking one of Mai's throat lozenges, thinking it might help her get to sleep.

She must have dozed off shortly, however, because the next thing Laura knew, she awoke to a light tapping on the door. She sat up to find the room bathed in a late-afternoon glow.

Snatching her robe from the end of the bed and tying it around her body, she went to the door, opening it just a crack.

"Laura, I'm sorry, I seem to have overslept," Miguel confessed through the two-inch gap. "It's almost five. You both must be ravenous. How does an omelette sound to you ladies?"

"Fine for me, but Mai just wants to sleep," Laura whispered. "And if she wakes up later, maybe some broth and toast would be better for her stomach than eggs. Give me a couple of minutes to get dressed. I'll just leave her a note in case she gets up while I'm eating."

"OK, meet you in the kitchen. Go through the living room and turn right, you can't miss it."

After Miguel left, Laura pulled on the pair of linen slacks she had packed and topped it with a bulky sweater. Checking that Mai's breathing wasn't congested or labored, she scribbled a message on the pad she kept in her purse and propped it on the nightstand next to the bed.

Leaving the bathroom light on and closing the door most of the way to cut down on the glare, Laura quietly let herself out of the room.

Walking slowly back down the long corridor she had rushed through a few hours ago, she noticed that the hall was lit by a strip of spots attached to the ceiling. They focused on the tile floor and on several picture frames that displayed photographs and paintings.

The photos were mainly of Indian girls, dressed in exquisite native costumes. The same lovely faces were represented over and over again, and Laura noticed a definite family resemblance between the young girls.

Miguel had the same high cheekbones and straight black hair. Laura tried to remember what he had said about his family. But she couldn't come up with anything. He had told her nothing about his background, beyond the information that his ancestors had been Mexican and Irish and Indian.

Indian themes certainly dominated the artwork in the long hallway. When Laura examined the oils and watercolors, she recognized the signatures of some very famous Southwestern painters. It appeared that Miguel was a serious collector of fine New Mexican artwork.

This was borne out when she got to the living room. There were several more paintings hung on the two long side walls, along with tapestries and brightly woven rugs. Miguel, however, had used most of the wall space to display pottery. Accent shelves held dozens of beautifully crafted pots and water jugs. Laura remembered seeing similar pieces in the Pueblo Indian section of the museum she and Mai had visited in Albuquerque.

Her eyes traveled from shelf to shelf, until reaching the far end of the room where she discovered the most beautiful pots in Miguel's collection exhibited on a twelve-foot high stone wall.

Looking like something an anthropologist might find when he finally got to heaven, each piece nestled in a deep niche carved out of the ledge rock. Some of the pots had been painted with subtle desert colors. Others were black or ocher, but somehow burnished to a metallic sheen.

The impact of the pottery—the love and talent that the

artists had invested in their creations—almost over-whelmed her. But it was not the beautiful claywork that made Laura's eyes fill with tears.

As her gaze darted hungrily around the treasure-filled room, what she felt most strongly was a great sense of peace. The wondrous sensation of having come home at last. It seemed that Miguel had somehow gotten inside her head and discovered her perfect idea of "home".

A sense of *family* radiated from this room. Laura pic-tured teenagers listening to their newest tapes, stretched out on the soft woven rugs scattered over the golden planked floor. She could almost see Miguel sitting on one of the large leather chairs, enfolded by its plump arms, while he put a youngster on his lap and retold a favorite fairy tale.

And when Laura's eyes discovered a fireplace in the far rock wall, she imagined lying on the alpaca hearth rug with Miguel—to be warmed by the heat of burning wood and then scorched by the fire he provoked in her blood.

Laura shook her head, trying to clear it of scenes that would never be. She was aided when the tantalizing aroma of sautéing onions and herbs began floating through the room. The scent helped her remember that she had been on her way to find the kitchen.

She forced herself to walk directly through the living room, without stopping every few feet to touch a pot or feast her eyes on a stark desert landscape. Instead, she followed her nose until she located the L-shaped dining area and kitchen.

Turning the corner, she almost ran into a ladder tilted against the wall. Carved from pine—with its rungs tied to the rails with rawhide—the ladder might have been used to enter a Pueblo kiva at one time. But here, it led up to a sizable loft, cantilevered over the dining area.

"Fantastic," Laura mumured. But when she lowered her eyes, she realized that the word also described the lean, rangy man who moved deftly around the kitchen, dressed in wickedly tight jeans and a brightly checkered shirt.

The smells of food cooking might have lured her in here, but the sight of Miguel's long-muscled thighs in stretched demin caused Laura's mouth to water.

She must have made some sort of sound, probably a moan of desire, because the staccato clicking of his western riding boots on the russet terra-cotta tiles abruptly stopped and he swiveled to face her.

"Ah, *querida*. Come in, come in. *Mi cocina es tu cocina*." Miguel's voice was low and husky, as he called her into his kitchen, with a variation of the traditional Spanish phrase of welcome.

"A—anything I c–can do to help?" Laura stuttered, when his beautiful green eyes delivered another jolt to her raging hormones.

"Just belly up to the table for the best omelette this side of Albuquerque. Hope you like hot food."

"Hot as in temperature, or hot like in temperament?" she asked. Did she really have the brain power left to make a joke? Amazing!

Michael threw back his head and laughed at her wordplay. "I guess it's a little of both. I just wanted to warn you that the jalapeño peppers can be a bit much for the uninitiated."

"Well, don't worry about me. Since moving to California, we've learned to love them—even Marthe. In fact, she's tried adding them in some of her German recipes, and let me tell you that the results are verr–rry in–terr–rresting," Laura said, imitating her housekeeper's accent. "Just let me get some water, in case."

She took one of the tall glasses on the table to fill at the kitchen tap.

"Better use the bottled stuff in the refrigerator," Miguel warned. "We're on Delta water here, and with the years of drought we've had the salt levels are way up."

"Oh. Gee, I've never thought about the sodium content

before. Everybody in Los Angeles seems to drink some sort of designer water, but I guess I always thought it was a status thing. Maybe I should check out our own water quality when I get home. Do you want a glass, too?'' she asked when she passed his place setting on her way to the refrigerator.

''I'd rather have one of the Dos Equis you'll find somewhere in there,'' he said.

Laura filled her glass and located the Mexican beer Miguel wanted in one of the door shelves. She saw an opener hanging on a nearby cabinet and placed it next to the bottle at the table.

Michael watched her doing the mundane little action and a swelling of happiness made a lump form in his throat. She looked so right in his kitchen.

Maybe that was because he had been thinking of her when he redesigned it and decorated the rest of the house. That long-ago night in Ecuador, they had talked about the kind of home they would own one day. And even though it had seemed like a foolish fantasy, when he finally found the perfect house two years ago Michael tried to include everything Laura wanted.

Turning toward the stove to pour the omelette mixture into the heated frying pan, Michael fought hard to dampen his wildly oscillating emotions. He wanted Laura so much. Beyond the passion they had shared last night, he wanted her in his life . . . permanently.

But as he carefully used a spatula to lift up the setting portion of the eggs and allow the still-liquid part to run underneath, Michael felt that too-familiar sensation of skeletal fingers dancing on his spine once again. And he knew that his grace period was almost over.

He couldn't wait any longer. After they finished eating, he would tell Laura about Kattie and the kids.

Michael's hand paused in the process of scattering grated cheese over the eggs. The more he thought about it, the more he felt sure that Laura would understand about last night. When she realized how much he loved her—had always loved her—she would forgive him for the sin of omission he had committed by not telling her that he was engaged.

In the long run, absolving him of that error might be easier for Laura than facing the fact that he would always have to be available to help Kattie and her children, if they ever needed him.

Maybe Laura would understand better if he told her just what they had done for *him*, when he had been so desperately unhappy two years ago.

When he met Kattie and the kids, he had been at a low point in his life. Oh, his business had become a runaway success and for the first time he had money to burn. Yet, he had absolutely no one who really gave a damn about him.

His mother and sisters long ago had given up on his ever returning to Taos. Ironically, he longed for them to come to California, if only to visit occasionally. He wanted to show them what he had achieved—his research lab, this house.

Yet, no matter how many letters he wrote, or how many plane tickets he sent, his family refused to come here.

Two years ago, Michael spent most of his days in a sterile laboratory and his nights in an apartment that was just as lifeless. When he started sleeping at the lab, he finally acknowledged that he had to do something drastic or he would be on his way to a complete breakdown.

The solution didn't involve psychotherapy. Michael decided that his salvation hinged on making a real home for himself. And since he couldn't bear the idea of going back to Taos, it would be in the San Francisco area.

He wanted a house that was within commuting distance to his lab in Concord, but still out in the country, with a mountain behind it and a stream nearby. He envisioned a home with thick, solid walls and a fireplace in every room to keep it warm. Warm enough so that the hunk of ice his soul had become might have a chance to melt.

The real estate agent finally found just what he wanted. An added bonus turned out to be the Sinclair family. Kattie and her four children lived next door. Michael learned later that they had moved into the rundown rental house only months before, just after Kattie left her husband.

The lot of them charmed Michael. Kattie made outrageous jokes about everything, including her plight as a single mother. And the kids immediately accepted him as a friend.

Over the next year or so, they slowly filled empty places in each other's lives—Michael, Kattie, and her children. Yet, up until a few months ago, Michael never thought of the cheerful little brunette as anything but a good neighbor. And he really didn't believe that Kattie felt any differently.

Then Jeff went through a rough time, and Michael seemed to have some answers that helped the boy work out his adolescent problems. Suddenly, Michael seemed to be spending more of his free time in the Sinclairs' home than at his own place. Kattie invited him over almost every night for dinner, and gently coerced him into going along to baseball games and school events.

Michael hadn't minded at all. Slowly, he found himself looking at life, at the kids—at Kattie—in different ways. Oh, bells didn't ring the first few times he kissed her, but he felt a definite pleasure in the quiet warmth she generated in him.

Yet, they had never made love. Kattie was a little embarrassed when she admitted that, although she had moved away from the Ozarks at seventeen, the strict morals she learned in the hills and "hollers" of her youth were still in force. She just couldn't sleep with a man who wasn't her husband.

Although he stopped seeing anyone else, Michael didn't push Kattie. Even after she accepted his proposal of marriage, they decided that with so many children underfoot the honeymoon would be the right time for their first intimacy.

How could I have been so blind, Michael wondered, savagely twisting the burner dial to the off position. Turning the omelette onto a platter, he remembered how Laura had looked this morning, all rosy and moist from the loving they had shared. He had every reason *not* to make love with her last night, but none of those moral inhibitions had stopped him.

The feelings Laura generated in him were absolutely unique in his experience. He had been compelled to kiss her; he had burned to embrace her. Last night, he just *had* to fuse his body with hers. There hadn't been a question of choice. Like his next breath, loving Laura had been vital to his continued survival.

No, neither Kattie's unbringing nor his nobility had kept Michael from her bed. The truth of it was, there had never been any love to express in the first place.

Affection, yes. Respect, of course. Liking, definitely.

But nothing like the desperate need he had to keep Laura in his arms, his bed . . . his life.

Michael looked down at the omelette he had made and thought about the process. It was very much like his life at this moment. He had finally gotten together all the proper ingredients to make it perfect, but unless he did everything just right, the only thing he would wind up with was scrambled eggs.

TEN

With shaking hands, Michael took the platter to the table. After cutting the omelette in half with a serving spatula, he retrieved a salad from the refrigerator and cornbread from the oven.

Laura watched Miguel present the meal he had prepared. His movements were quick and sure, as if he had done this a thousand times in the past. And perhaps he had. Judging by the high-tech kitchen, maybe he often cooked for himself and a guest. Most likely, that guest would be a woman. A woman who would ignore the food and feast her eyes on the leashed masculine beauty of his body, which was exactly what Laura did now.

When he sat down at his place, Laura was so captivated by the innate grace of the simple action that it took several ticks of the clock before she became aware that he was watching her watch him.

"Well, shall we dig in before it gets cold?" he asked, when she dared meet his eyes.

In her embarrassment, Laura felt her cheeks grow hot. Looking down at the food in confusion, she found that her appetite had fled, chased away by a more compelling need. Forcing herself to stop playing with the fork, she put a tight rein on baser hungers and tried to do justice to the meal.

After the first bite, it wasn't that hard to do. The omelette tasted delicious and the cornbread teased her tongue with the piquant mingling of a sweet batter and the spicy bite of peppers. The jalapeños were potent enough for Laura to go through three glasses of water, but Miguel's one beer seemed sufficient to protect his tongue from their ravages.

"Absolutely wonderful," Laura mumbled, while biting into another slice of the cornbread.

"An old family recipe," Michael said lightly, but he secretly felt pleased with the wholehearted way Laura attacked the meal. Her bones might be as delicate as a hummingbird's, but her appetite was pure condor.

"You know, I've found that besides the people I've had to leave behind when I've moved, it's the food that I miss the most about a place," Laura revealed. "Washington had some great Chinese restaurants that I think about sometimes. And remember that drink they made in Ecuador. You know, that little green fruit they whipped to a froth and then served chilled."

"*Naranjilla*!" Michael provided the name from his photographic memory. "Yeah, I miss it, too. And my mother's fry bread and a stew she made called *posole*. She also ground blue corn for terrific tortilla chips and . . . and she made lots of other things I haven't tasted for years."

Laura sat absolutely still, trying not to breathe too loudly while Miguel reminisced about his mother's cooking. He was opening up to her for the first time.

But even as that thought formed in her mind, a shadow darkened the green light in his eyes and he abruptly pushed back his chair.

It is time, Michael thought, *time to make a clean breast of the past to Laura, and to find out if I have any future worth living for*.

"Why don't we just leave the clean-up until later?" he

said out loud. "I've got some coffee brewed and we can have it in the living room."

Carrying mugs of aromatic coffee, Miguel led Laura to a sofa set in front of the large stone fireplace.

Trying to lighten the somber mood that had followed them into the room, Laura rushed into a humorous anecdote as soon as she settled into the deep cushion of the couch.

"When I taught in Washington, D.C., one of my friends on the staff had a great story about jalapeño peppers," she began. "He was a Spanish teacher . . ."

As Michael settled on the other end of the sofa, he knew that he should interrupt Laura—to tell her another kind of tale. One he was sure would not cause her upper lip to curve with the hint of devilish mischief, like it did right now.

But he couldn't bear to stop her, to break this mood. It might be the last time Laura ever wanted to share a remembrance with him, and he devoured every word, every subtle movement of her beautiful, expressive features.

Laura felt the details of the story she had been sharing skittle away under the impact of Miguel's intense attention. The need she saw in his green eyes left her with the feeling that there was no other woman in the world he wanted to spend the next hour with. Or, perhaps, the next century.

Yet, when she waited an expectant second for him to say something, or to reach out for her, he just sat there and then gave her a nod of encouragement.

Taking a deep gulp of her coffee, she cleared an imaginary frog from her throat, pretending that was the reason she had interrupted herself—and not the call of wayward hormones. Forcing a cheerful smile on her lips, she began again.

"As I said, my friend, Guillermo Espinoza, is a Spanish teacher. What else would he be with a name like that, right? But actually, Gil is a native New Yorker. And his ancestors were Sephardic Jews from Spain, who came to America to escape from persecution not too many years after the Pilgrims landed.

"Anyway, Gil said that when he first began to work teachers could take a year's sabbatical after each decade of service. When he earned his first leave, he convinced the board of education to let him go to Mexico and live among the people, rather than take the traditional route as an exchange teacher or sign up for advanced university studies.

"So, he and his family drove to the west coat of Mexico in a camper and set up on one of the beaches just north of Acapulco."

"Really roughing it!" Miguel put in.

"Yeah, tough," Luara echoed. "But according to Gil, they avoided the tourist traps and made friends with the local fishermen—one family in particular. The Calderóns introduced Gil to the challenge of the jalapeño. They took great delight in seeing him sweat and his face turn red, trying to be one of the boys. This went on for weeks. They found hotter and hotter peppers, which of course they could eat right down to the stem, seeds and all. Gil tried to uphold gringo honor, but he was well on the road to an ulcer. Then he remembered a bit of trivia he had read somewhere, and he devised a plan for revenge."

"And, what did he do?" Michael asked, finding himself caught up in Laura's account. It was like watching her on the stage again. She had the ability to set a scene, drawing her audience into it with the sound of her voice and the force of her personality. She must have been one hell of a teacher.

"Well, it cost a fortune, but he called home and had his sister arrange to send down the makings of a dish that was a part of *his* family's ethnic culinary arts.

"When the package arrived, he and his wife got to work—making gefilte fish. They bought some fresh lake carp and pike. Then they cleaned and finely chopped the fish, mixing it with shredded carrots and matzoh meal, which was one of the ingredients Gil's sister had sent down.

"After the fish patties were boiled and then chilled, they invited their Mexican friends over for a feast and presented the fish as the main dish. Everyone was ready to eat when Gil brought out the special sauce that went with it.

"He showed them how to cover the fish with the bright red stuff, and then demonstrated how good it tasted by taking a great big bite. His wife and children also dug in. From the way the kids were giggling, the Calderóns knew something 'fishy' was up. But, of course, they were guests and they couldn't offend their hosts.

"Well, after one taste of gefilte fish—and the freshly prepared horseradish—they were all running around trying to find enough water to put out the fire in their sinuses. The Calderóns accused Gil of trying to poison them, but calmed down when he explained about the article he had remembered reading.

"It seems that people can get used to eating even the hottest food, such as chili peppers. Yet, when they try something out of their experience, such as horseradish, the tongue is super sensitive to the new irritant. Well, when everybody realized that the joke was on them, they all laughed and sat down to finish the meal.

"According to Gil, after that feast everyone in the fishing village grew to love horseradish. When their stay ended, the Espinosas presented their friends with starter plants of the root. And Gil says that to this day the Calderóns serve the best gefilte fish in all of Mexico."

Michael laughed in soft appreciation of the punch line. He reached over to tug on the bobbing curl of Laura's hair that had been tantalizing him all through dinner and her storytelling.

He had only meant to tease, but at the feel of that blond silk, his fingers took on a life of their own, smoothing a gentle caress on her bright head. Laura gave a strangled little moan and turned her lips into his palm. The warmth of her mouth on his skin caused an instant reaction in his loins, and Michael felt himself quicken—hard and fast—like a randy teenager.

With as little thought for the consequences of his actions as a seventeen-year-old might have, he pulled Laura onto his lap. Her mouth welcomed his invading tongue, and her nipples tightened into tiny jewels at his touch.

Groaning with the knowledge that he was seconds away from losing control, Michael surged to his feet with Laura securely held in his arms. He stalked across the floor, intent on getting her up to his bedroom before he had to take her on the floor.

When Miguel backtracked toward the kitchen, Laura's eyes widened in bewilderment. She wanted to make love as much as he obviously did, but did he plan to use the dining room table? She felt relieved for a second, when he bypassed that piece of furniture. But when they stopped at the skinny wooden ladder leading to the loft, Laura belatedly figured out that was where his bedroom must be located.

"Miguel! Have you gone out of your mind? You can't carry me up there," she protested. Not that she didn't like the fantasy of being swept up to that gabled loft by a modern-day Tarzan. But she definitely was not Jane. In fact, she had always been plagued by a phobia about ladders, and had never been higher than the second rung of one in her life!

At the panic in Laura's voice, Michael froze. Then he understood. She was worried that her daughter might wake up. How could he have forgotten about Mai, sleeping down the hallway? But even worse, how could he have let himself come to within seconds of betraying Laura's trust yet again?

As the heat sizzling in his blood ebbed, a chilling realization traveled up his spine. It was obvious that he was a man who didn't have the force of will to honor a pledge he had made to himself.

Slowly letting Laura slide from his grasp, Michael rested his head on one of the ladder rungs and squeezed his eyes shut. This moral fugue of his had to stop right now.

"Laura, please accept my apology for acting like a caveman," he said, turning to see the confusion on her face. "Would you come back to the living room with me? There's something I've been meaning to tell you since last night, and it can't wait a second longer. Just give me your promise that you'll hear me out completely before you make up your mind."

Without even waiting for that assurance from her, Miguel stalked back to the living room, leaving Laura to stand alone and afraid.

She had never seen his eyes look like that. The beautiful deep green had turned murky, like the sea before a hurricane. And the sound of his rich, husky voice had gone dry and raspy. What had he just said? To hear him out before she made up her mind? About what?

As Laura slowly walked back to the living room, her brain made an intuitive leap. And that small flame of hope she had felt earlier, glowed noticeably brighter. He was going to ask her to marry him!

When she saw Miguel standing by the fireplace, rubbing the back of his neck, Laura almost blurted out that she didn't need to be persuaded. She would marry him in a minute. But he turned to look at her, and what she saw in his eyes was not passion. It was more akin to pain, or fear.

Sinking down onto the same couch they had abandoned so precipitously just minutes ago, she watched Miguel pace in front of the hearth, like a green-eyed panther measuring the confines of his cage. After two or three minutes of the relentless activity, he abruptly stopped in front of her.

How to begin, Michael wondered, looking down at Laura. She returned his gaze and he swallowed hard at the trusting encouragement he saw in her eyes. If he had the time, he could come up with a thousand ways to tell her about Kattie.

But maybe it was best if he went back to the beginning, the *very* beginning. Sighing deeply, Michael finally sat down on the edge of the couch next to Laura.

"*Querida*, have you seen the pictures around the house? The photos of the girls in Taos Indian costumes."

Laura nodded, although she felt a bit lost.

"They're my sisters, actually, my half-sisters."

"Half-sisters?" Laura echoed, her confusion total now.

"Yeah. After my father died in a car accident, my mother married Will Montoya and they had the three girls."

"I thought I saw a certain resemblance to you in their pictures. But I don't understand, Miguel. That first day we met at the University of Maryland, didn't you say that you came from Albuquerque, not Taos?"

The image of Miguel, and the dark corridor where she had crashed into him, was as vivid in Laura's mind as if it had happened today, not seventeen years ago.

"It seems that I'm not the only one who remembers the exact details of that first encounter," Miguel said, with a smile that didn't quite reach his eyes. "But to answer your question, I went to college in Albuquerque. And I told you I came from there because I felt more at home in that city than I ever did in all the years I lived in the Taos Pueblo.

"Look, Laura, I know it's confusing, but I have to tell you about my life growing up in the Pueblo, and how I've been trying to find a real home since I left there. Just bear with me, and then I hope you'll understand what happened last night at the hotel."

Understand? How could she understand anything when Miguel talked in dark riddles? She wanted to stop him, to make him backtrack to the point where she had gotten lost. But he was speaking so quickly, so intently, that Laura didn't think he would even hear her plea.

"It started when my father, Ramón O'Brian, visited the Taos Pueblo for the first time. He came from Chamisa, a town near Santa Fe. It's a community of artisans, mostly of Mexican stock, mixed a bit with the Irish who helped build the railroads.

"Dad was a mixture of both races. His eyes were colored like mine, but his hair was light brown and he was even taller than I am.

"He also had the gift of gab and seemed to be able to bring out the best in people. Since he was a potter, he tried to express that goodness in the pots he created. One day, he felt compelled to go to the Taos reservation to see if they would teach him how they made their pottery."

Michael gestured to the large, gleaming urn flanking the fireplace.

"That one's from the Pueblo. They use a special kind of clay with mica in it."

"Clay?" Laura asked, completely caught up in Miguel's story. "I swear, even this close, it looks like some kind of metal." She fought the urge to get up and run her fingers over the shiny surface.

"No, the sheen is from the mica. When the finished pot is sanded and fired, it turns out like that. My father wanted to try the technique in his own work. Well, my mother's people were potters, experts in using the micaceous clay. And you can imagine what happened next."

Laura smiled, and Miguel nodded.

"Right . . . love at first sight. Anyway, Dad, with his Irish gift of blarney running on high, somehow worked himself into that closed community, and into my mother's heart. Not only did he get permission to study the secret techniques, the council of elders even gave its blessing for him to marry my mother . . . with certain reservations . . ."

Laura groaned, but when Michael studied her face, he saw that she was grinning.

"Hey, no pun intended," he chided, realizing that she was only reacting to his last sentence.

"OK, you're forgiven, but try to be more careful in the future," Laura responded, delighted that Miguel's mood had brightened perceptively when he talked about his parents. She had been afraid he was going to reveal something horrible. "Well, go on, what were the reser—ah, what were the conditions for their marriage?"

"Just that the council made sure Dad understood he would never have any right to the land held in my mother's name. They also decreed that any children who came along would have to be brought up under the strict guidance of tribal custom."

"And how did your father react?"

"Well, owning property had never been high on Dad's list of priorities, and he really admired how the Taos Pueblo elders tried to preserve the old ways. So, he agreed. My parents got married and lived happily ever after. At least until I was born."

Michael stared down at his clenched hands, bitterness replacing the affection in his voice.

"Actually, I didn't give them much trouble until I reached seven or eight. Then I started questioning everyone and everything. I just didn't understand all the rules I was supposed to follow. Like wearing boots with the heels broken off and not cutting my hair. Or having to slice out the seat of my trousers and then needing to cover my . . . ah, pride, with a blanket wrapped around my waist."

Michael's head snapped up when he heard the strangled little sound Laura made. "Hey, you're not mocking ancient Indian customs, are you?" he challenged with counterfeit severity.

"N–no, never," she managed to say around another bubble of laughter. "So, did you really wear your hair long and your boots with the heels off . . . and everything else?"

"Just the hair."

"You wore it . . . in braids?"

He nodded reluctantly. "Yes, *querida*, I had long braids until I turned sixteen and went off to college."

A picture formed in Laura's mind of Miguel standing on a high desert mesa with his waist-length hair freed to furl like a blue-black flag in the wind. By sealing her lips together, she barely stopped herself from suggesting that she just might be ready to take a crack at climbing that ladder now.

Instead, Laura expressed a safer notion, one that made her amber eyes dance with mischief.

"Ah, Miguel, I wish you had kept your hair long. It'd be wonderfull to slowly undo those braids and use my fingers to comb them out. And when you leaned over me, I could feel the weight of it all along my . . . Oh, excuse me, darling, I didn't mean to interrupt you. Please go on and tell me more about the Pueblo."

Michael threw back his head and laughed hard. She had cleverly reversed that romantic stereotype of a man lusting to release a woman's passion by letting down the length of her confined hair. He recalled wanting to do that to the chignon Laura had worn earlier.

Yet, even though she was teasing, the picture she evoked in his mind was so sensual, so erotic, that for the first time in twenty years, he actually regretted cutting off his braids.

But when he took a deep breath to regain his control, Michael abruptly remembered that there had been a deadly serious purpose in telling Laura about Taos.

Sobering in an instant, he hurried to finish his story. "All right, Laura, I'll tell you the rest of it. I felt as if I was living in the stone age. Besides the customs I just told you about, we didn't have any electricity. And we had to fetch every drop of water we used in the house from the river, in a tin bucket.''

"Not even running water?" Laura said, unable to stifle her shock.

"Yeah, water in buckets and drafty outhouses. And the only good thing about no electricity was that the outline of the Pueblo against the sky didn't get ruined by a lot of silly looking TV antennas.''

"Speaking of television, I probably didn't miss much not having one. But a teacher hooked me on science fiction, and some of the kids at school told me about 'Star Trek.' That program seemed to symbolize all I was missing; a whole universe of information was denied to me because I lived in the Pueblo.''

Laura reached out and put her hand on Miguel's arm in sympathy for the unhappy boy he had been. How different from her own life at that age.

Her father had actively encouraged her to stretch her mind. He was always asking fascinating questions, or giving her puzzles to solve that had Laura scurrying off to find answers at the library or in a museum.

It was a wonder that Miguel's intellectual curiosity hadn't shriveled and died an early death in the desert of the mind he described.

"How did you finally break away?" she asked quietly, when Miguel seemed to have become lost in his past.

Michael shook his head and rubbed his neck. He was nearing the end of this painful explanation and his muscles screamed with the tension he felt.

"My father died," he finally said. "And, although he had given the elders his word, I refused to undergo initiation. God, my mother was so disappointed in me. She really believed in her religion and felt terrified that I would call down divine retribution.

"But when I begged to be sent to the Indian boarding school in Santa Fe, she gave in and let me go. From that point on, I went home as little as possible. For brief vacations, and not even then after I won a series of summer scholarships for advanced university study."

"Your mother must be a very special woman, to let you go like that . . . especially with your father gone. She must have been so lonely." Laura felt her eyes start to burn and turned away from Miguel's searching gaze. She thought about how bereft she would have felt if Mai had left her right after Jerry died.

"Oh, no one has to be lonely in a pueblo. It's like living in a huge extended family. But even if that hadn't been the case, about the time I went off to school my mother married Will Montoya."

Laura looked carefully at Miguel's face to see how that event had affected him. He surprised her with a wide smile.

"It was probably the best thing that could have happened to her . . . and to me. He's a great guy, although it took me a few years to figure that out. And since Will was a member of the governing council, my mother got back into the mainstream of Pueblo life. She had her responsibilities to her religion—and to her daughters when they came along. Oh, she didn't forget me. For years she tried to get me to come home. But I never could, at least not to live.

"After the Peace Corps and the army, I studied for a doctorate at Stanford. When I decided to set up my research company, I found a great location in Concord. But even then, I still wandered, spending a lot of time on business trips and living out of a suitcase."

"Like I've been doing this last year," Laura murmured.

"Yes, but I'll bet your apartment is a real home, and that you and Mai and your housekeeper are a real family. What I came back to was a bed and four bare walls."

"But, but . . ." Laura gestured to the living room, where warmth radiated from every carefully decorated corner.

"Yes, this house. This house is where all my rambling

through the past has been leading, Laura. Two years ago, it dawned on me that my life was an empty shell, and I needed a home. I found this place, and I worked and worked until it was just right. Yet, even then, it wasn't enough.

"Oh, it looks like a home, it smells like a home, but you can't create a home out of beautiful decorations. A home is family, and that's what has been missing here."

Michael took both of Laura's hands in his and willed her to understand.

"*Querdia*, I didn't know it until recently, but I needed a woman I could love, and who could love me. I want kids I can watch grow and help become wonderful human beings. And that's when I finally found . . ."

"Oh, Miguel," Laura breathed, "darling, I understand."

He *was* asking her to marry him. She was the woman he loved, and who loved him. He would get to know Mai; he'd learn about all her lovable qualities and the special talents that made her unique.

And perhaps he wanted more children; Laura could give him those children, who would be a product of their special love.

"No, Laura, you do *not* understand. But there is something that you must never forget. I have always loved you, I've never stopped loving you. Even when we were separated, and you got married, I couldn't forget you. Yet, there came a time when I had to give up fantasizing about a life with you. There came a day when I knew that I had to find a real life for myself.

"And it happened about five months ago. Laura, there's a family who lives next door . . ."

"Kattie and her kids," Laura whispered, trying not to give in to the whirling black spiral that plucked at her consciousness.

"Yes, Kattie, and her son Jeff, and her three daughters—Lisa, Mary and little Amy. They've been my neighbors for two years, and well, you see, they needed a lot of help. Broken pipes, and . . .''

''Miguel, just tell me straight out!'' Laura demanded.

But she really didn't need to hear any more. She knew what was coming. Yanking her hands out of his grip, Laura got to her feet and backed away from the couch.

Miguel held out a shaking hand toward her. ''Laura, I asked Kattie to marry me five months ago.'' He rasped the terrible words she had feared. ''But you've got to believe me, Laura. That was before . . .''

A sudden commotion outside left him with his mouth hanging open. He was halfway off the couch when the front door burst open, and a beautiful little whirlwind entered the quiet room.

''Mickey, Mickey? It's Kattie. I'm back!''

ELEVEN

Laura craned her neck around a large lamp to see a small, lovely woman—with dark, windblown hair and a big grin on her face—extract a key from the lock. Right behind her, three little girls, stair-stepped miniatures of Kattie, piled into the room and ran into Miguel's arms.

Kattie was only a step behind. She reached over her daughters, way up, to wrap her arms around Miguel's neck. The kiss she plopped on his mouth was full of enthusiasm.

"Kattie? You were supposed to be gone two weeks, not two days!" Michael managed to mumble around the stranglehold she had on his neck.

"Two days were all I could take, darlin'. Oh, Mickey, I missed you so much. Let's not wait 'til next month to get married. Let's trot on up to Reno tomorrow and find us a justice of the peace."

"Mom? Mom, what's all the racket. People shouting woke me up, and I feel rotten."

Everyone in the living room swiveled toward the hallway where Mai stood, leaning against the doorjamb, her thin little body looking too frail to hold her up.

Hastily moving away from the huge table lamp, Laura

hurried to her daughter. Putting a steadying arm around her shoulders, she felt Mai's forehead with her free hand.

"Mickey, who in the world are they . . . that little girl, that woman? And what are they . . . ?"

"Kattie, this is Laura Nord—ah, Easten and her daughter Mai. Mai has a possible strep infection and inflamed ears. I took her to see Dave Green this morning, and he won't let her fly home. So, they're staying here until . . ."

"Whoa, there. You better start over again, Mike," Kattie said, sounding amused even amid her confusion. "I seemed to have missed a few paragraphs from this story."

Blocking out the man standing so close to Kattie Sinclair, Laura looked into the woman's blue eyes and filled her in on the information she wanted. At least all the facts Laura could impart in front of four little girls.

"What Mig—ah, Mike, means is that we knew each other in the Peace Corps, in the bad old days. We ran into each other by accident in San Francisco, and he took pity on us when he saw how sick Mai was. The doctor said that really serious complications might develop if we flew back home to Los Angeles, and he advised us not to travel until the antibiotics have a chance to work."

Having given that explanation, Laura turned and led Mai to the couch. Finding an afghan on a nearby chair, she took it and wrapped the warm blanket around Mai's shoulders.

"Oh, the poor little thing," Kattie said, abandoning her death lock on Michael's neck to cross the room and sink down on the other side of Mai. "Amy had strep last winter. In fact, the children's clinic where I work was swamped. Hurts like the dickens when you swallow, honey?"

Mai nodded her head, and grimaced when she attempted a gulp to prove her point.

"Well, let me make you something that's guaranteed to soothe that throat. I was just back home in Arkansas, Laura, and my Ma reminded me of all the herbs we used to collect each spring to dry and make into home remedies.''

She looked over to Michael. ''I brought some for you to analyze, Mike. Did you know, Laura, that Irishman over there is an expert in making miracles out of native cures? Aren't you, Mickey, honey?''

''Ah, well, we've done a lot of research into the plants that our ancestors used for medicines,'' Michael said softly, when both women looked at him. Kattie's glance was full of pride. Laura's seethed with contempt.

He knew that she would never forgive him. If only Kattie had returned a half hour later . . . even ten minutes. But she hadn't, and now he had to figure out how to deflect the amber-edged daggers Laura's eyes were throwing at him.

''Oh, I'm sure *Mickey* is wonderful in using all the old knowledge. Great herbalists—the Celts,'' Laura agreed, trying to keep the rage she felt out of her voice.

It seemed that green eyes weren't the only thing he had inherited from his father. *Mickey O'Brian also knows how to lay on the blarney real good,* she thought cynically. Lord, why had she listened to him last night? How could she have believed anything he said after what happened in Ecuador?

''Well, let me get to work,'' Kattie said cheerfully, rolling up the sleeves of her blouse and picking up the large carry-all she had dropped at Michael's feet. ''Kids, why don't you take Mai back to her room, while I boil up some of these leaves. Mai, how old are you?''

''Eleven,'' Mai said as she stood up.

''Oh, good. You're right between Lisa and Mary.''

''I'm Lisa, and I'm twelve-and-a-half,'' the tallest girl said, taking Mai by the hand.

''And I'm going to be eleven in September,'' Mary informed her, grasping the other one.

''Well, I'm Amy, and I'm six,'' Laura heard the youngest pipe up as the group disappeared down the hallway.

When she turned back, Kattie had already moved into the kitchen area. With the ease born of long familiarity, she opened the cabinets and drawers to extract a pot and a strainer, along with various sized mixing bowls.

"Laura, I'll explain everything later," Michael said under the noise of banging pots and running water. "Just remember that you don't know everything."

"Nor do I ever want to," Laura hissed at him.

Michael tried not to flinch when he saw what was in her eyes. He had hurt her so badly . . . yet again. He wanted to reach out, to hold Laura and rock away the anguish that lay under the rage in her eyes. But since *he* had caused that suffering, Michael knew it would be better if he kept out of her way for a bit.

"I'm going to the stable to take care of the horses," he said to the room in general before grabbing a flashlight and stomping out the kitchen door.

No, I guess I don't know everything, Laura thought to herself, watching his broad back disappear into the night. *I don't know much about men, that's for sure. I would have bet my soul that the man who touched me so ardently last night had meant every endearment, every declaration of undying love.*

Indeed, she *had* bet her soul. She had used it as the stakes for her future with Miguel, along with her body and her heart.

No, not Miguel, never again Miguel. He's Michael, or Mike, or Mickey O'Brian now. *A hundred percent Irish,* she bitterly reminded herself. Well, it didn't matter anymore what she called him. Kattie was welcome to her Mickey. Let her deal with that cheat and liar.

Michael seemed to make a habit of betraying women. Maybe it was a macho power game with him. It must give him a high, some sort of rush.

Poor Kattie. Laura looked over at the woman working so industriously in Michael's kitchen. She seems like such a nice person. Maybe I should go in there and tell her what really happened last night. Oh, I won't hurt her with the gruesome details, but I should warn her about the man she's so desperate to marry.

After a moment's thoughts, Laura decided that it was not her place to warn Kattie about Michael. The woman had been his next-door neighbor for two years, his fiancée for five months. And in day-to-day contact, Kattie must have spent a hundred times more hours with Michael than Laura ever had.

If Kattie hadn't seen his fatal flaw by now, there wasn't much Laura could say to convince her that she was involved with a loser.

Well, one thing for certain, Laura knew that she would have to get out of his house. It might be too late to drag Mai out tonight, but the first thing in the morning Laura would locate a motel.

"This really should cook for a couple hours more, but I'll strain some of it off to give to your daughter right now," Kattie said over her shoulder.

Laura gathered together her tattered mental resources and went over to see what sort of concoction Kattie had prepared for Mai.

"Ah, Kattie," Laura said, clearing her throat when she looked down into the bright green liquor that the woman had just poured into a sieve-capped glass. "Kattie, I don't think . . ."

"Oh, I know what you're thinking. This crazy hillbilly is out to poison my child. Really, honey, this is tried and true, something that's been used for hundreds of years. Want me to give a swig to Amy first?"

"Oh, I didn't mean . . ."

"Here, I'll drop an içe cube in to cool it, and then you try a teaspoon. You sound a bit hoarse yourself."

Laura tried not to grimace when Kattie offered her a taste of the elixir. But the cooled liquid went down with surprising ease. It *was* soothing, and left the slightest hint of mint on the inner surfaces of her mouth and throat.

"That's wonderful, Kattie. I'm sorry if I doubted you."

"No, don't apologize. It's hard to take anyone on faith these days, isn't it? I think that's what I like so much about Mickey, his word is good as gold. Oh, my, did some of that go down the wrong way?"

Kattie patted Laura's back until she managed to stop choking.

"It's OK. I'm all right now," she assured the dark-haired woman.

"Good, I was worried that maybe a leaf had gotten into the filtrate. Now, what was I saying? Oh, yes, about trusting Mike. Well, after my experience with J.J., it took me the longest time to believe in any man. J.J. is my ex-husband. Lord, I don't want to remember how stupidly I behaved about that man and his promises."

Kattie stood looking at Laura, a hint of catlike curiosity seemed to dance in her blue eyes until she finally blurted out, "Couldn't your husband come with you on this trip?"

"My husband is dead. He died of leukemia three years ago," Laura said tersely.

"Lord, I am sorry. I've got such a big mouth. And such a nasty imagination. Like when I came in and found you and Mickey here together. Well, what I thought was really very bad of me. But like I said, I should have remembered that if Mickey were to tell me that the Pope is Protestant, well, then I'd . . ."

Laura never learned the extent of Kattie's faith in her fiancé. The sweet, haunting sound of violin music coming from the other end of the house robbed the woman of her voice.

With maternal instinct telling both of them something was wrong, they followed the lure of the music to its source and rushed to the guest bedroom Michael had assigned to Laura and Mai.

The Sinclair girls were sitting in a row on one bed, while on the other, Mai played the violin, her slight frame moving in concert with the ebb and flow of a solo excerpted from the Tchaikovsky Violin Concerto. Among the most heartrending themes ever created in symphonic music, the emotions Mai wrested from the strings wove around the room, capturing the very breath of each person in her small audience.

When she finally stopped, on a high, aching note of profound loneliness, several long seconds passed before anyone moved. Then Laura crossed the floor and sank to her knees in front of her daughter.

Looking at her mother, Mai carefully put her violin back in its case, and then wrapped her arms around her neck, her body shaking with sobs.

"It's all right, it's all right," Laura crooned, rocking the child back and forth. "Is your throat worse, sweetheart? Are you feeling bad?"

"N–no. My ears and t–throat are better," Mai said. She swallowed hard, making a tremendous effort to control her anguish and sat up. "It's just that Lisa and I were talking about not having our fathers around, and I got so scared. *That's* why I took the bus to San Francisco this morning.

"I didn't want to worry you or Marthe, but I had this awful dream last night. You were here in San Francisco, in a tall, tall building. And it started shaking and swaying, like that ride at Universal City we went on. But in the dream, the walls fell down on you. Oh, Mommy, what if I lose you, too!"

"Hush, baby, hush," Laura said, trying not to lose control in front of her daughter. "It's going to be all right, Mai. I promise you that this is the last trip I'm going to take without you. I'll talk to the company president and see if they have something for me to do in the home office. Even if they don't, I'll work something out so that we can be together all the time. I give you my word."

When Mai began sobbing with relief, Laura gave up trying to stem her own tears.

From his place in the doorway, Michael squeezed his eyes shut. Oh, this was such a mess. He longed to take

Laura and Mai into his arms, to tell them not to worry, that he'd take care of everything from now on. But then he opened his eyes and saw Kattie sitting on the bed, her arms hugging her own girls to her body.

Michael remembered that not five months ago, he had made just the same sort of pledge to the Sinclairs. He had given them his word to always be there when they needed him.

His eyes rose to the ceiling. And in his imagination, his gaze pierced the plaster and then the clay tiles covering the roof to search the heavens. He marshaled his thoughts, and did what he hadn't done since he was eight, and his father lay dying on white hospital sheets.

Please, if you're up there, let me find a solution for all of us. Please!

Michael didn't know if he was pleading for the intercession of his father's saints, or asking for aid from the more capricious *kachinas* of his mother's people. But he opened his heart and soul for examination, and hoped that his true intentions would find favor with whatever entity might hear his prayer.

"Hello in there. Is there a problem?" A loud male voice coming from the other end of the hallway rose above the sound of Mai's sobbing.

Michael leaned out of the doorjamb and saw a stranger in the corridor. The dark-haired man had the short, wiry body and bandied legs of a boy jockey who had outgrown his profession. Seeing Michael, he hesitated, and then slowly approached.

"The kitchen door was standing wide open and I heard crying. Sorry to bother you, but I'm looking for your neighbor, Kattie Sinclair. Do you know where she is?"

"No, oh God, no," Kattie suddenly whispered inside the bedroom. "Don't say anything, Mike. Don't let J.J. know we're here!"

Completely confused, Michael did nothing for crucial

seconds, time enough for the man to move down the hall with surprising speed.

"Kattie," he cried, looking around Michael's shoulder. "Kattie, kids? What in the world are you doing in there?"

"Daddy! Daddy," a duet of high, feminine voices squealed. The two oldest Sinclair girls jumped up and threw themselves into their father's arms, while the littlest one peeked shyly from the safety of her mother's lap.

As Laura watched, Kattie put her six-year-old on the bed, then she marched over to the doorway and defiantly linked an arm through Michael's.

Her cool, clinical voice had none of its soft, deep-woods accent when she addressed her ex-husband. "What I am doing is none of your business, J.J. Sinclair. How dare you follow me back from Arkansas? I told you this morning, when you showed up at my mother's house, that I didn't want anything more to do with you. Ever!"

"You didn't let me explain, Kattie-did. I'm a new man, I'm cured!"

"Now, haven't I heard that one a dozen times or more? And didn't I always believe you? Sure, like a darn fool, I did. But when we lost the house that last time, I swore I wasn't going to be your enabler any more."

"Kattie, I've done what you always wanted. I've gotten counseling and joined a self-help group. Just like you've been telling me to do for years."

"A day late and a dollar short, like always," Kattie continued in that cold voice. "Actually, you're two years too late."

"But I didn't know where to find you all this time. Your ma and kin wouldn't tell me diddly. If my cousin George hadn't been keeping an eye out, like I asked, and called me when you finally went home to visit, I probably never would have found you."

"Well, that would have been OK with me. We've got everything that we need here. I have a good job at a local hospital. And glory be, I found out that a nurse's salary may not be anything like what you make training horses, but it's enough to pay for our food and housing and everything else—now that there isn't someone robbing us blind with his betting.''

"Oh, sweetie, I know I was a rotten, sick fool. But I swear, I haven't placed a wager on the ponies in over two years.''

"Betting on greyhound races now, are you? Or is it football and baseball, or the Oscars?''

"Kattie, I'm not betting on anything. Why can't you believe me?''

"Because I'm too old for fairy tales, Jeffrey Jeramiah Sinclair! Or maybe, it's because I've found a real man.''

Kattie finally seemed to realize whose arm she was holding, and she looked up at Michael. "Mickey, darlin', meet my ex-husband, J.J. Sinclair. J.J., this is Michael O'Brian, my fiancé. We're getting married in a day or two. Right, sugar?''

Laura watched with detached interest when Michael's skin first paled, and then picked up a deep bronzed tint on his high cheekbones. He suddenly glanced up at the ceiling, and then threw Laura a cryptic smile.

"Oh, I'd say the gods were planning a wedding or two real soon.''

"My God, Kattie,'' J.J. Sinclair gasped, looking up at Michael's grinning face. "You must be joking. You're just punishing me for all the misery I brought to you. I understand how angry you must feel, but it'll be different now. I want to take care of you. I want to be there for you . . .''

"Be there for me? No! It was Michael who was here last winter, when Amy had strep throat and a hundred and four temperature. *He* was here to teach Mary how to ride a horse. Where were you, when the kids at school razzed Jeff about playing the piano and he wanted to give it all up? You were probably in a bookie joint, putting your rent money on some broken-down longshot.''

"No, I was spending that money on a psychologist—and on all the detectives I had looking for you, you mule-headed, ornery woman!"

"Well, if that's how you feel, you have my permission to leave."

"I'm not leaving until you come to your senses. I have the right to see my children. That divorce decree gave me visiting privileges. Privileges that you denied me when you abducted our kids."

"Abducted? I just decided to move out here and get a new start. I didn't make any secret of where I was going."

"Then how come your ma and everybody else in Tanner's Creek wouldn't tell me where you were?"

"I didn't ask anyone to keep my address a secret. Ask *them* why they wouldn't say anything."

"I did," J.J. said, shamefaced. "Everybody at home, except cousin George, said that you'd be better off without the likes of me. But that's not true anymore. And I finally convinced your mother of it because this morning she told me where you lived. Kattie, you've got to believe me, too, and give me another chance."

"Oh no, I don't. Children, come help me get the bags out of the car and into our house. Mickey, darling, be a treasure and see this man off your property."

"And when you're free, *Mickey*, would you let me use your phone to make reservations at a motel and call a cab?" The words just popped out of Laura's mouth, but she suddenly knew that now was the time to get Mai and herself out of this three-ringed circus. "You have a wedding to plan, and we'll just get out of your hair."

"Over my dead body, you'll leave!" Michael snarled the words so vehemently that everybody just stared. But he didn't care. The gods were in his corner for a change, magically conjuring up J.J. Sinclair. So Michael was going to do his part to work out this mess. "You have no right to take Mai to a motel. It'll be noisy, and who knows what kind of beds they have, or what kind of people will be next door."

What could be worse than sleeping in the same house with a man who specializes in breaking hearts, Laura wanted to shout back.

"Mike's right, you have to think of what's best for Mai," Kattie said softly, defusing Laura's anger.

"I just don't feel right staying here any longer," Laura protested, her eyes darting between Mai and Michael.

"Then I'll tell you what we'll do. You bundle Mai up and we'll take her over to my house. The beds have new mattresses, and you'll even have a pediatric nurse to keep an eye on your daughter real cheap."

"Kattie, that's wonderful of you, but . . ."

"Not another but. Too many butts around here already," she snapped, giving her ex-husband a lethal glare.

Somehow, in less than a quarter hour, Laura had repacked their things and found herself in the room Lisa and Mary shared, tucking Mai into the lower level of a bunk bed.

"Where will you girls sleep?" Laura asked, her eyes looking warily up to the top bunk she had been assigned.

"Oh, we both have sleeping bags and can just spread them out on the floor, here. Right, Mai? We'll all have a great time."

"The only time Mai is going to have is the sleepy variety," Kattie said, entering with a tray holding a bowl of chicken soup and a measure of the green elixir she had prepared."

"Aw, Mom," Lisa groaned. "Mai was going to tell us about all the movie stars she's seen in L.A., and where she got her striped haircut. It's just the kind I've always wanted, Mai."

"Well, you can stay while Mai has her supper, then she's going to sleep. And you two are going to Jeff's room to sack out there," Kattie directed. "Come on,

Laura, let's leave these ladies to talk about things we're too young to hear. I'll make us a cup of coffee.''

Laura smiled at the girls, who were already avidly questioning her daughter about life in Tinsel Town. She turned to follow Kattie to the kitchen.

She found her looking into a cupboard, and then examining the contents of the refrigerator. ''Bare as Old Mother Hubbard's,'' Kattie said, over her shoulder. ''Would you mind holding the fort while I run to the supermarket for some coffee and the fixings for breakfast?''

''Why don't you let me go?''

''Nonsense, it's only half a mile down the road, and I know the store's layout. It won't take me twenty minutes to get the stuff.''

''Then I insist on contributing to the groceries,'' Laura said. ''Let me see the bill when you get back.''

''OK, fair's fair. Anything special you like or Mai hates?''

''No, she's not a picky eater, thank God. Marthe, my housekeeper, is a great believer in the clean-plate club. Oh, speaking of Marthe, would you mind if I called her on my charge card? I really should tell her that we'll be staying here at least until Monday.''

''Sure, no problem. Well, I'll be back in a jiffy,'' Kattie said, fishing car keys from her purse on the way out of the kitchen door.

Going to the wall phone, Laura dialed home and then talked briefly with Marthe. She reassured her that Mai was in good hands and, before saying good-bye, she gave her housekeeper Kattie's telephone number.

After hanging up, Laura felt strangely restless. She paced the room, vaguely noting that like the rest of the house it was immaculately clean, but rundown. Except for the full-sized concert grand piano in the living room, the place was bare of everything but the essentials.

Laura knew how much time and money it took to keep

ahead of chaos in a house. And it was obvious that Kattie had little of either precious commodity.

Neither did Laura. She would have even less of the green stuff when she stopped lecturing and earning the added bonuses that went with all the traveling. Just thinking about her tenuous finances chilled her. Finding that her hands were freezing, she opened cabinets to see if Kattie at least had the makings for a cup of tea or cocoa. She finally spotted a box of herbal teabags.

Taking one out, she ran some water into the kettle she found on the stove. After turning on the gas flame, she located a cup and stood waiting for the whistle.

Her eyes were on the spout, but her attention was focused three hundred yards away, on the man next door. How could Miguel have been so deceitful? He hadn't said one word about a woman in his life last night, when they met for drinks, or later, when he escorted her to the hotel room.

And she had asked! She remembered sitting on his lap, feeling so incredibly happy to be in his arms again. He had said that he wasn't attached.

No, to be truthful, she had asked if he was married. Not if he might be taking the plunge next month, or the day after tomorrow.

Just a minor detail he hadn't thought it necessary to reveal. She would never had made love with him, knowing that he was not free. She wouldn't have, would she? No, it might have been the hardest thing she had ever done— moving off his lap and making him leave—but she would have done it.

Oh, he was the lowest kind of bastard! He had told her that he loved her, again and again, and seemed to prove it by the fever driving him. There had been moments last night when Laura feared that they were going to set the bedding on fire with the passion that blazed between them.

But now, instead of building a life together, Miguel was

out of her reach again. He, like almost everyone she had ever loved, had left her . . . alone and hurting.

Logically, she knew that her mother and Jerry hadn't wanted to die. And her father certainly didn't plan the tragic decline of his vast mental powers, which had sealed his mind behind an impenetrable wall. But the end result was the same. He had left her, too.

Laura had conquered the primitive rage she had felt. The unreasonable feeling that if her parents and husband had really loved her enough, they never would have abandoned her.

But there was nothing irrational about her anger at Miguel O'Brian. He had really abandoned her . . . twice. In Ecuador, he had questioned the force of her love for him, thinking that it was a shallow emotion to be cast aside for the slightest reason. And now, after making her believe they would finally have a life together, Miguel had abandoned her again to marry Kattie Sinclair.

Under any other circumstances, Laura would applaud his choice. Kattie and her girls were delightful, and Laura couldn't work up any emotion but sincere liking for the self-named "hillbilly".

The steam funneling out of the kettle condensed into a cheerful whistle that seemed at odds with Laura's thoughts. Switching off the heat, she poured the water over the teabag and dunked it until the color looked right.

Sitting down at the scarred, family-sized trestle table that dominated the kitchen's eating area, Laura wrapped her fingers around the cup, trying to draw some comfort from the heat that radiated through the stoneware.

Miguel. The name echoed again and again in her thoughts. There was no Miguel anymore, but try as she might, Laura found she really couldn't think of him as Michael either. Not that it would be a problem much longer. After Monday, she would never see him again.

The liquid in her mug almost sloshed over the brim,

when the kitchen door flew open and J.J. Sinclair burst into the room.

"Kattie, sweetie, you have to listen to me." The man skidded halfway across the floor before he realized that the woman sitting at the table was not his wife. He did a comical doubletake, and then his eyes darted to every nook and cranny of the room. Laura had the feeling that he was about to get on his hands and knees to check under the table, when a sound behind him made J.J. whirl.

But instead of his ex-wife, Miguel O'Brian stood in the doorway, his face a drawn, harsh mask.

_____ TWELVE _____

"Sorry, folks, but the woman you want has gone grocery shopping," Laura informed both men.

"She's gone? Where does she usually shop?" J.J queried.

"Haven't the foggiest, Mr. Sinclair," Laura said.

"About half a mile west, the big Safeway on the right," Michael supplied, and quickly moved to the side when the smaller man dashed out, his grateful thank you floating behind him.

"Do you think it's wise, telling him where she is?" Laura asked.

"They have things to discuss, and being in the middle of a supermarket might help keep their emotions from getting out of hand," Michael replied, the hint of a smile on his lips.

"I guess you're right. They do have to get the details of visiting rights settled. Those girls really seem to love their daddy, and I guess he loves them, too. Well, I'll leave you here to wait for Kattie," Laura said, very pleased with the adult way she had handled this unexpected meeting.

But before she had a chance to get up from the table, Miguel had shut the door and moved across the room.

"I didn't come over to talk to Kattie," he said. "I wanted to talk to you. To apologize . . ."

"Oh, no need to apologize for last night. You didn't have to twist my arm to go to bed with you," Laura interrupted. "And don't worry, I didn't spill the beans to Kattie. I like her too much to hurt her in that way. She'll probably have plenty of opportunity in the future to find out just what kind of man she's married."

"I wasn't going to apologize for last night," Miguel bit off. "I'll never be sorry for those hours you spent in my arms." He advanced on Laura, taking her shoulders in his hands.

"Let me go," she hissed, not wanting to scream and bring the children into this scene.

"No, now that I've found you, I'll never let you go again," he grated.

"Well, buddy, you obviously have a problem. There's a wedding taking place real soon, and I'm not into adultery. I'm not stupid enough to have anything more to do with a man who has the morals of a slug."

"Oh, there's going to be a wedding real soon, but it won't be Kattie I'm marrying. It'll be you."

"Like hell, I'll marry you," Laura grated between clenched jaws. She tried to pull away from his grasp again, but he just yanked her to her feet and wrapped his arms around her until she stopped her futile struggling.

"Ah, Laura. Please, sweetheart, just listen. Listen to what I tried to tell you this afternoon. Kattie and I have been friends for a long time, over two years. We were a couple of lonely people, who helped each other out whenever we had problems. We got along great, me and her and the kids, and it slowly dawned on us that marriage could be the solution to all our needs.

"But, believe me, *querida*, the moment I saw you yesterday afternoon I knew that even if you just said hello and good-bye to me, I could never marry Kattie. Because I didn't love her like a husband should love a wife. Like I loved you, and always have loved you.''

Michael felt the trembling in Laura's shoulders, and he realized that she was sobbing. He tilted her head up, but she wouldn't look at him. She stubbornly kept her eyes shut, as if she couldn't stand the sight of him.

"Laura, please hear me. I love you, and as soon as I ask Kattie to release me, I want to marry you.''

"Please take your hands off me." That low, tortured whisper had an immediate effect. Michael automatically opened his arms and Laura backed away. The table stopped her before she had moved three inches, but the fear in her eyes when she finally looked at him, kept Michael from reaching out for her again.

"I can't ask you to leave your fiancée's house, Miguel. But until Mai is well enough to travel, I will ask you to have the decency to leave me alone. I don't think Kattie's trust should be violated in her own home. I'm sorry I had any part in hurting her last night, but that sin is wholly on your head.''

"You don't believe me," Michael whispered.

"No, I don't believe you. I was a fool to believe that cockamamy story about lost letters and Machiavellian government interference in our pathetic little lives. And I was stupid to believe you last night, when you implied that you were free as a bird and, oh, so happy that we were together at last. But I will never let you make a fool of me again.''

Michael stood there, watching his life end as Laura walked out of the kitchen. He knew that he had the hard evidence to prove to her that he hadn't been lying about those letters locked in his desk next door. But what was the use? What kind of man would he be, if he had to beg for her love?

* * *

Laura stood outside the girls' bedroom, struggling to compose herself before she entered. In between the huge gulps of air she pulled into her lungs, she could hear the children chattering away.

"I hope Dad and Mom get back together," Mary said, "I really miss him."

"Well, I don't," Amy piped up. "I'm glad that Uncle Mike is going to marry Mommy. He's lots of fun. He came to our first-grade Halloween party, and . . ."

"Are you sure Mike is going to marry your mom?" Mai interrupted. "This morning in the car, I saw him . . ."

In the hallway, Laura cringed, wondering just what her daughter had seen.

Curiosity filled Lisa's voice. "What? What did you see, Mai?" she asked.

"Never mind, maybe I was mistaken. Go on, Amy, what about the Halloween party?"

"Mike came instead of my Mommy, 'cause she had to work. He helped us make real Indian masks. And he told us all sorts of scary stories, about witches called *yiapana*, who chase people on winter nights. But he gave us all a special black stone you can carry to keep them away. Mai, I bet you didn't know that Mike is part pebble Indian."

"That's *Pueblo* Indian, you dork," Lisa scoffed. "That's why he's so dark. Gran'ma said his picture gave her the shivers when Mom showed her the one we took at Great America last summer. She said he reminded her that the Cherokees killed her great-grandfather back in the old days."

"Oh, what does Gran'ma know?" Mary broke in. "She's never been fifteen miles from Tanner's Creek, and . . ."

"She doesn't have to go anywhere. People come from all around to get herbs from her and to buy her violins," Lisa scolded her middle sister. "Mom told me Jeff inherited his musical ability from Gran'ma."

"Your brother plays the violin?" Mai asked, her voice alive with interest.

"No, he bangs away at that classical stuff on the big, old piano in the living room. Didn't you see it when you came in? He's going away next year, to Juilliard. That's why he didn't come to Arknasas with us. We were going to be there for two weeks, and he has a job starting on Monday to help make spending money. But except for that, the school isn't going to cost Mom a nickel, 'cause he won a big scholarship in a contest."

"Where is your brother? I'd sure like to talk to him."

"He's fishing. But he'll be back tomorrow."

"Good, I want to ask him all about Juilliard. Gee, I'd give anything to study there." Laura heard Mai let out a deep sigh. "But even if I won a scholarship, I couldn't go. My mother doesn't have anyone else but me. And I won't leave her alone."

"Did your Daddy leave you, too?" Amy asked with a six-year-old's lack of tact.

"No, don't you remember I said that he died when I was eight. He had leukemia, and was awfully sick with it for seven years. He really tried his hardest to fight it off, with radiation and all sorts of experimental treatments. But nothing worked for long."

A long silence followed that revelation.

Laura felt torn between going into the room and taking Mai into her arms, or going back down the corridor so that Mai wouldn't see her mother's fresh tears.

Deciding to sit in the darkened living room for a few minutes, Laura retraced her steps down the hall. Her eyes automatically glanced into the kitchen, when she passed it.

To her surprise, Miguel was still there. He sat at the table, his proud, straight back slumped and his eyes staring blindly at the wood grain in front of him.

Deep lines she had never seen before etched his lean

cheeks, giving him a haggard, drained look that instantly reminded her of how Jerry had appeared late in his illness.

Perhaps it was her vulnerable state of mind, because of the conversation she had just overheard, but Laura found that she just couldn't bear to see Miguel in such obvious pain.

No matter what he's done, I just can't leave things as they are, Laura thought to herself. Her step was silent on the kitchen carpeting, but his head snapped around even before she placed a comforting hand on his shoulder.

"Miguel, whatever has happened, I want you to know that I wish you only the best in your life. And I'm glad that you've found somone like Kattie."

Miguel looked into her eyes and then placed his long fingers over hers. "Oh, *querida*, what have I done to you? I'm so sorry for all the misery I've caused you . . . in Ecuador and here. Please forgive me."

He stood, towering over her. A hint of moisture had clumped his thick black eyelashes into short, spiky rays. Laura saw whatever agony she felt mirrored in Miguel's clear green eyes.

Her hand rose to capture the single tear that had traveled down the seam that etched his cheek. He groaned at the touch, and pulling Laura to him, his mouth claimed hers.

Her cry of protest instantly turned into a sigh of defeat. To her, he was temptation incarnate, and she seemed to have absolutely no willpower where he was concerned.

Laura's arms wrapped tightly around his waist as he moved back to brace his hips against the table. His legs formed a vee just wide enough so when he drew her closer, she nestled tightly between his thighs.

It was madness, yet Laura could no more resist the whirling sense of danger his kiss promised, than she could have stopped the earth from turning on its axis.

In desperation's grip, Michael somehow knew that he only had minutes—seconds—to prove to Laura with his body, what he had failed to make her believe with his words.

He tried to touch her everywhere, to communicate with his fingertips and mouth and tongue how much he loved her—only her. But he almost came undone when he lifted her sweater, and his lips informed him that Laura was braless.

His whole body shook like an aspen in a windstorm when he found that her nipples could hardly wait for the attention of his tongue.

Laura spun out of control at the sight of Miguel suckling. at her breast. Her fingers trembled as she wove them through his thick, dark hair and pressed his head tightly against her body.

Yet, even though blood pulsed in her ears in concert with the movement of Miguel's lips, Laura somehow heard the squeal of two cars braking to a sudden stop near the curtained kitchen window.

Michael heard the commotion, too. With a guilty groan, he pulled down Laura's sweater and pushed away from the table. Outside, angry voices joined the harsh sound of car doors slamming, but Laura had already moved to the sink, and Michael dropped into one of the kitchen chairs.

Kattie and J.J., their arms full of grocery bags, piled into the kitchen a second later. They were so involved in their argument that neither one seemed to notice Laura splashing water over her face, or Michael arranging his chair so that his lap was covered by the table top.

"If I've told you once tonight, I've told you a hundred times, J.J., there will be no reconciliation. You can have your lawyer call mine and work out visitation rights. But you make sure to let him know that you can only see the kids, not me. You will pick them up on my doorstep and drop them off, and not try to come inside to talk to me."

"Why, Kattie-did, that sounds like you're afraid of me. Maybe you're too scared to trust yourself alone with me because you remember how good it was between us."

He ran his fingers up her arm and then gave a dark curl of hair a little tug. "Well, I remember, sweetheart. Like that time we rented the motel suite with that motorized bed and all the mirrors . . ."

Feeling like a voyeur, Laura desperately grabbed the tea kettle and turned the water on full blast to fill it.

"Do you need any help putting away the groceries?" Michael said at the same time, trying to keep his grin from splitting his face.

"Oh . . . oh, Michael. You're h—here!" Kattie stammered. "Well . . . good. I wanted to talk to you. Mickey . . . we, ah, never got to talk about tomorrow."

"Tomorrow?" Michael echoed.

"Yes, don't you remember, we're going to Reno to get married," she reminded him. "We'll fly up early and be back in just a few hours. Maybe Laura would babysit for us. Come on, Mike, come to my bedroom where we can have a little privacy."

She glared at J.J, then tugged at Michael's hand, leading him down the hall.

Laura just stood there, kettle in hand, staring at the retreating pair. She squeezed her eyes shut blocking out the image of them walking out of the kitchen together. Miguel had never said one word to contradict Kattie. He still planned on marrying her!

"Damn stubborn, stubborn woman," J.J. muttered, picking up a grocery bag and putting perishables into the refrigerator.

"Ah, would you like some coffee or tea?" Laura managed after a long minute.

"Coffee's fine, Laura. Here's some instant," he said, handing her a new bottle.

Laura went through the motions of making two cups of coffee, feeling like the newest member of the walking dead.

"What's between you and O'Brian?" J.J. asked, when he finally sat down to drink the hot brew.

"Oh, there's n—nothing between us . . . nothing. We

were in the Peace Corps together years ago, and just happened to run into each other again.''

"Hogwash," J.J. said pleasantly. "You're long gone on each other."

"Mr. Sinclair!" Laura said, halfway rising from her chair.

"Sit down, missy. I'm not making any moral judgments here. You both seem like real nice people. I got to talk to Mike a bit over at his place a while ago, and he's real solid folks. Even though he looks like a red Indian."

Laura just stared at the man. What kind of people did they raise in Tanner's Creek, Arkansas?

He had obviously read the expression on her face and patted her hand. "No offense meant. Got a bit of the Cherokee in me, myself. What I meant was, for all her flighty ways, Kattie seems to have picked herself a fine man. But she'll never marry him."

"She won't?"

"Nope, the lady still loves me . . . I can tell. Just going to take her a bit of time to admit it."

"Mr. Sinclair." Laura laughed shakily. "*You* may not realize it, but your ex-wife is down the hall, in her bedroom with the man."

"That's true. But I'd bet you my last dollar . . . ooops, forget I said that. I mean, I'm not worried. I'd say they've not slept together. Kattie wouldn't have changed that much in two years. Needs to have the ring first," he said with utmost confidence.

Laura shook her head. How in the world could any woman resist Miguel O'Brian?

"Dad, Daddy!" Lisa ran into the room and threw herself into her father's arms. "Daddy, you're still here." Mary hit her father's open arms a second behind her sister.

"Darn right, I am. And now that I've found my sweet peas again, I'm not going to let them out of my sight again. Where's my youngest petunia?" He looked around and spotted the six-year-old in the doorway. "Come on, Amy, give your old dad a big kiss."

But Amy just stood there, shaking her head.

"Just like her mom, that one. Well, I'll bring both of them around." J.J. predicted.

"Oh, Mrs. Easten, Mai wanted you," Lisa said from her station by her father's side. "She said that she's tired and wants to talk to you before she falls asleep."

"Thanks, Lisa. Well, goodnight everyone, I think I'll make a night of it, too."

Laura slowly went down the hall, thinking over all that J.J. Sinclair had told her. Miguel and Kattie hadn't slept together, he said. Somehow the thought made her step lighter.

She walked down the darkened corridor toward the room she shared with Mai. That door stood wide open, shedding light on the hallway carpet. Another door was partly opened, a thin crack of illumination making a bar on the rug. Laura glanced inside with natural human curiosity as she went by. She only got a glimpse of a mirrored bureau, but the reflection in the glass made her stagger and almost lose her balance.

The mirror showed two people sitting on a wide bed, arms tightly clasped around each other. Laura stopped for a paralyzed minute while she saw a copper-colored hand gently caress dark-brown curls.

"You're wonderful, Kattie," Miguel said in his deep, husky voice. "I'll see you in the morning at breakfast, and we'll tell everyone our news then."

A few minutes earlier, Michael had entered Kattie's bedroom and looked around. He had never been in it before and was surprised to see that it was so spartan.

Except for pictures of her four kids and the intricately pieced together quilt that covered the bed, there was no hint of personalization. It seemed that deep in her heart, Kattie felt this wasn't really home.

They talked about that, along with the fact that both of them had just realized they were in love with other people.

Kattie cried, but when she finally raised her head from his shoulder, she was smiling.

"Thanks for listening," she said. "Just talking it through sure helped me get my head straight. I'm too wiped out to handle the stress tonight, but bring J.J. over for breakfast in the morning and we'll tell everyone at the same time that we're not getting married. That should clear the way for you and Laura."

"It should, but given my luck, I'm not going to count on clear sailing with her," Michael said ruefully.

"It won't be easy for me, either. But still feeling like I do about him, I've got to give J.J. another chance to prove himself."

"If only Laura will do the same," he sighed.

"Well, from what little you've told me about what happened in Ecuador, the woman does have cause to question your commitment to her."

"Oh, I have proof I told her the truth about what happened back then. The problem is what happened today." *And last night*, Michael said to himself. He hadn't told Kattie anything about the night he and Laura had spent together. But it seemed that she was a lot more observant than he had given her credit for.

"Just tell her you love her so much that you couldn't stop yourself last night," Kattie advised. "That is what happened, isn't it?"

Michael just stared at her for a long minute. He finally nodded, giving Kattie an affectionate hug and her hair a playful tousle. "You're wonderful, Kattie. See you in the morning, and we'll tell everyone our news then."

Michael's head snapped around. Was there someone out in the hallway? He thought he had heard something that sounded very much like a gasp of pain. But by the time he got to the door and fully opened it, the long, dark corridor was empty. Shrugging his shoulders, he waved goodnight to Kattie and went toward the kitchen to collect J.J. Sinclair.

THIRTEEN

It was the smell of bacon that finally enticed Laura to open her eyes. The bedroom door opened a second later, and Laura looked down from the top bunk to see her daughter and Lisa Sinclair enter the room.

"Come on, Mom, breakfast is going to be ready in a few minutes. You should see the pancakes Lisa and I made. Kattie said the bathroom is free and that you can take a quick shower. Mom, we're starving," Mai insisted, when it appeared that her mother just wanted to pull the covers over her head and go back to sleep.

"All right, I'm up. But should you be out of bed? How's your fever?"

"Kattie just took my temperature. It's almost normal and my ear hardly hurts at all. Mom!"

"Be there in ten," Laura said, carefully turning on her stomach and then stretching her legs down until her feet touched the lower bunk. Once safely on the floor, she headed for the shower. *Boy, I could use a tenth of Mai's recuperative powers,* she thought, while standing under the hot water. Her daughter was well on the road to recovery, but her own status was not as hopeful.

Laura hadn't slept much last night. Part of her sleeplessness was due to her distrust of the safety rail on her upper berth. But mostly, she had stayed up thinking about the last thirty-six hours of her life, and experiencing a gamut of emotions.

Denial, anger, bargaining, resignation, acceptance.

She had gone through similar stages of grief after losing her mother and Jerry.

Laura hadn't lost Miguel—he had never really been hers to lose. But she had grieved last night, just the same.

First, she denied that anything really important had happened between them. She told herself that many women had casual romantic encounters and were none the worse for them.

That rationalization quickly gave way to anger. Anger at Miguel for giving her a dream of love again, and then cruelly transforming the fantasy into a nightmare.

But even having been betrayed by him, at some point in the night Laura found herself making bargains with some supreme being, asking that Miguel change his mind about whom he was going to marry.

As Laura had carefully changed from one position to another on the mattress, she entered the next stage in her grief. Resignation. She had become resigned to the fact that she would never find true fulfillment with Miguel, that she would have to learn to live without him once more.

And now, as she towel dried her hair and braided it into a long rope, she reached the final step in the healing process. Acceptance. She would go into the kitchen and smile. She would smile at Kattie—because she was a nice lady, who had not done anything wrong. And she would smile at Miguel—because she loved him and wanted him to be happy.

The big kitchen table was crammed to capacity when Laura got there. Everyone turned to look at her as she entered, smiling.

"Good morning. Can I help you, Kattie?" she asked, knowing that her voice sounded over-bright.

Kattie hesitated a second, then said, "Sure thing, the bagels are warming in the oven. Would you put them in that bread basket?"

"Bagels?" Laura questioned, even as she filled the container and brought it to the heaping table.

"Right, we decided to have an all-American feast," Kattie proclaimed. "The girls made the pancakes, J.J. brought home-smoked bacon from Arkansas, Mickey's mother sent him some sort of Indian salsa for the eggs. And I think there's nothing better than bagels and cream cheese to round out this nightmare in cholesterol. But, hey, how often do we break and make engagements around here?"

Kattie sat down next to her ex-husband, leaving Laura to sink into the only available chair, next to Miguel. She looked dumbly across the table at Kattie, not sure what the woman meant. But before she could pose the questions that trembled on her lips, J.J. had a question of his own.

"Mike here was tellin' us about his time in the Peace Corps, and I remember you saying that you were in it, too. Must have been a wonderful experience . . . helpin' people like that, right?"

Laura couldn't keep from glancing sideways at Miguel. His green eyes met hers and from his grin Laura knew he had experienced the same thing as she had over the years.

People who had not "been there", in the Peace Corps just didn't want to hear the real truth. They had their own preconceived notions about events, and didn't want their illusions altered in any way. Laura had loved Ecuador. The beauty of the country, the wonderful people. But trying to teach there had been frustrating, for many reasons. And seeing the glint in Miguel's eyes, she understood that he had shared her difficulties with the system.

"Well, as . . . ah, Mike probably told you, working in the Peace Corps is something that a person can't forget.

Those two years in Ecuador still color my life, even after all this time," she finally said, drawing on all her skills of diplomacy.

"Do you ever hear from the people you worked with down there?" Kattie asked. "The Ecuadorians, I mean."

"Oh, I still write to the family I boarded with. And their oldest son came to stay with my husband and me in Washington, when Eduardo went to medical school. God, it's hard to believe that he must be nearly thirty now. He was just in high school when I lived in San Gabriel."

"How about the other Volunteers?" Michael asked. "I'm sorry to say that I haven't kept up. But have you heard from any of them?"

"Living in Washington, I got called by anyone passing through. So, yes, I've seen several people from our group, and some from the other projects that were going on at the same time. And guess who came to that big reunion a few years back!"

"Who?"

"Cheryl Ducaine and Carmen Rodriguez. Of course, they're both married now and have different last names. Do you remember them?"

"How could I forget Cheryl . . . or poor Carmen."

"Not poor Carmen, at all. You're not going to believe it, but not only did Cheryl learn Spanish real fast, but Carmen went all the way to Ecuador to become fluent in English!"

Michael chuckled at the look on Laura's face. He wanted to give her nose a kiss and hold her for a long good-morning hug, but she was still caught up in her story.

"But, that's not the best part. It seems that they actually became friends. Such good friends that after their tour was over, Cheryl moved to Puerto Rico and they opened a school together in a little mountain town. Cheryl's last name is Hidalgo now, by the way. So it seems that prejudice doesn't have to be a terminal condition. The cure is just getting to really know someone.''

"Maybe my company should look into patenting that remedy, *querida*," Miguel suggested, his smile toasting Laura to her toes. He reached over to give her hand a squeeze. The gesture seemed so right that it was a long second before she realized he had done it in front of everybody, and she belatedly snatched her hand away.

Her confusion multiplied when he just chuckled and looked over at Kattie. "Well, Mrs. Sinclair, I think it's time we made our announcement, right?''

"Right, Mr. O'Brian," Kattie echoed, and then scanned the table. "Folks, there's something Mickey and I want to tell you. Some of you will be happy to know that after the events of the last couple days, we have decided to call off the wedding.''

"I thank you, God," J.J. said loudly.

"Right on!" Mai beamed.

"Momma, momma, does that mean that you're married to Daddy again?" Mary asked, bouncing up and down on her seat.

"No, it just means that we'll all have time to be together and see if things work out between us.''

"But what about Uncle Mike?" Amy cried. "Won't he be lonely and sad without us?''

Everyone looked at Michael. He cleared his throat and held his arms out for Amy and put her on his lap. "No, honey, I won't miss you because you'll all still be next door. And we'll still be the best of friends.''

"But you won't have a wife or little girls in your house, like Mommy told us you needed.''

"Oh, that's what I do need, honey. But if Laura will consent to be my wife, I'll have all of you for my friends, and Mai as my daughter.''

There was no doubting Mai's reaction to that statement: she nodded her head enthusiastically. But Laura just sat there—stricken—her face pale and blank.

"*Querida*?" Michael urged. "Laura, I didn't plan to ask you like this in front of a crowd of thousands. But will you please marry me and be my wife forever and ever?"

Every eye turned toward her, every ear strained for her answer. Laura slowly looked into each expectant face before her amber eyes met bright green.

"Absolutely not," she whispered. "I will never be your wife."

Pushing back her chair, Laura got to her feet and burst out crying.

Kattie immediately went to her side, and putting an arm around Laura, she led her outside, away from the babble of half a dozen people talking at the same time. After handing Laura the paper napkin she had automatically picked up at the first hint of tears, Kattie just walked next to her without saying a word.

As Laura slowly regained control, she saw that Kattie had directed their rambling stroll around to the back of the property, where a shabby gazebo stood under the sweeping limbs of an ancient live oak.

Kattie wiped off a section of planking for Laura with yet another napkin, and then sat down, waiting for her to completely conquer her tears.

"So, you're not going to marry him, hmmm?" she finally said, when Laura gave her a watery smile.

"Oh, Kattie, you don't know. He's asked me to marry him before, and then just upped and deserted me."

"In Ecuador, yes. He told me about what happened when you were young."

Laura couldn't believe Kattie's calm acceptance. But then, she hadn't told her the most damaging information. "And when we met again two days ago, he lied to me!"

"Lied? Michael O'Brian lie? No way!"

"Originally, that was *Miguel Enrique Vincente* O'Brian, by the way, which is another sort of lie. Yet, you're right, he didn't actually fib to me when we ran into each other at the Sir Francis Drake Hotel. But he didn't tell me the whole truth, either. Miguel let me believe that he was free, and all the while he was engaged to you. I'll bet that's another thing he didn't tell you about."

"Yes, he told me about the night in the hotel."

"He *told* you?" That was the most shocking thing Laura had ever heard.

"Oh, he didn't reveal any details, but he did say that you had met there after not seeing each other in fifteen years. And I sort of figured out the rest."

"Well, could you trust a man who did that? Who could forget to mention that he was engaged, while . . . while . . ." Laura just couldn't go on.

"Laura, I want you to listen to me for a minute. Let me tell you a little bit about the Mike I've known for the last two years. When he moved in next door, I was intrigued by him. Oh, not in the way you think. He's a . . . striking man, but that's not why I was so fascinated with him."

Kattie bent over to pick up a wide oak leaf off the redwood flooring and examined it for a minute before continuing.

"I just couldn't figure him out. He was obviously wealthy, with expensive cars, and the horses, and all that fantastic decorating he did so fast. He also seemed to have a ton of free time to supervise the improvements he put in. At first I thought, Oh, oh, we have a drug lord next door. But then he helped my son with some sort of project, and we got to talking.

"I found out that he *was* into drugs, but only in the best sense. He owned a research company and made life-saving heart medications derived from native plants. And since I'm a nurse, and my mother is an herbalist, we talked some more. That's when I learned the reason he had so much free time to spend on his house. It was because he hadn't taken a vacation in ten years.

"Well, over the next few months, he helped us more

and more. And Mike began visiting so often that I slowly figured out he had to be one of the loneliest men I had ever met. Oh, he's got lots of friends. There were people coming by for dinner all the time. But all of them were associated with his business in one way or another. There didn't seem to be anyone who just cared about *him*, as a person, and not as the president of his company."

"What about his family? He's got three sisters, and I think his mother and step-father are alive," Laura said.

"Yes, I knew he has a family back in New Mexico. But they've never been here—not once—even though he decorated that lovely guest room for his youngest sisters. I think, subconsciously, Mike was desperate enough to try to bribe them into coming for a visit."

Laura felt her eyes burn and her heart throb with guilt as she listened to the compassion in Kattie's voice. She had wondered about that room; she had been puzzled about the brand-new clothing. But even when Miguel had talked to her about his half-sisters, she hadn't understood. She had been too wrapped up in her own pain to see his.

And she talked about loving the man! Laura bowed her head in agony while Kattie continued talking.

"Anyway, we all came to depend on him. And truthfully, I think he came to depend on us. Finally, five months ago, he asked to become part of the family. That's more or less how he put it. I was happy to receive his proposal in just that way. I had a wild passion with J.J., and look where that got me. When I lived with my ex-husband, I was afraid to answer the phone, or open the door because it might be one of his bookies, demanding payment for his latest losses."

"That must have been terrible for you," Laura said softly.

"Well, we all have that little black cloud raining down on our heads, don't we? I know that you've had your share of troubles. But to get back to Michael's proposal.

Right from the start, we both knew that our marriage wasn't going to be the lovematch of the century.

"But, Laura, even though I told him that I wouldn't go to bed with him until we were married, the minute I said I'd marry him, he stopped spending those weekends in San Francisco."

"Weekends? I don't understand," Laura said.

"Honey, the man's a man. He had lady friends in the city who . . ."

"OK," Laura interrupted. "I get the picture."

"Do you? Laura, he didn't pressure me, not once. But for over five months, he spent every weekend with me and the kids. He didn't even go on a business trip. He was either at his lab, or here."

"Until two nights ago," Laura said bitterly. Now she knew the reason Miguel had made love so passionately to her. He hadn't had a woman in almost half a year!

"Don't you see, that's how much you meant to him. The man's dying for a family. He really loves my kids, if not me. So, what do you think it took to make him endanger all that?"

"My God," Laura whispered, ashamed of what she had been thinking. The full impact of what Kattie had just said—of what Miguel had been so desperate to make her believe—finally hit her. He had jeopardized everything he wanted because they had met again.

"But what if J.J. hadn't come back?" Laura demanded. "What would Miguel have done about his commitment to you and your children?"

"I can't answer that, and you'll have to make up your own mind about what his plans were. But, Laura, even before J.J. popped up, I was having my own doubts about marrying Mike. Truthfully, it was the physical part of the marriage that was giving me the most problems. Honey, I was scared to death."

Laura just stared at Kattie. Not in her wildest dreams could she imagine a woman who wouldn't want to jump on Miguel's long sexy bones. Yet, she could see that Kattie was telling her the truth. She just wasn't attracted to him in a physical way.

"Maybe it was because you still were in love with J.J.," she offered.

"Maybe. But I think it was more. Who was it that said, 'What are we but the sum of our yesterdays.'?" Kattie didn't wait for Laura to hazard a guess. "It doesn't matter, but to me it means that I'll always be my mother's daughter and a child of the hills where I was born.

"And in those hills, we never saw a man as . . . different as Michael. If I took him home, he would be treated like an outsider . . . not trusted and even feared."

Laura thought she understood what Kattie was implying, and she had to respect the woman for being so truthful; even if she deplored the concept of prejudging someone because of their physical differences.

"I see your point of view, Kattie . . ." she began carefully.

"But you don't feel the same way. You probably grew up exposed to a rainbow of people. I realized that when I heard you at breakfast, talking about that Volunteer overcoming her prejudices. And, it's true that I've learned a lot about acceptance since moving away from home. I have friends with a variety of skin tones.

"But it doesn't alter the fact that when I revisited my hometown, I found out I could never *marry* someone so removed from my background. It's my failing, not Michael's. And I can't tell you how relieved I was to see you together last night, when I got back from Arkansas."

"But you demanded that the wedding date be brought forward, the minute you walked in the door," Laura reminded her.

"I was just running scared, having seen J.J. again, and with all the old feelings threatening to overwhelm me." Kattie chuckled ruefully. "Sorry. Guess I couldn't have arrived at a worse time for you and Michael."

"No, he was finally telling me about you," Laura said, remembering the involved, painful dialogue. "Well, Kattie, you've given me a lot to think about."

"Honey, you've got all the time in the world to think—about two days, if I judge Michael's mood right. Maybe less," Kattie said, nodding in the direction of the tall, lean man, who was striding purposefully toward them.

But Michael had not come to plead his case again. Instead, his eyes were full of sympathy, when he took Laura's hand in his.

"Laura, there's a phone call for you. Marthe gave Kattie's number to your father's nursing home in Arizona. He's had a stroke and they don't expect him to live."

FOURTEEN

After Laura ran into the house to talk to the nursing supervisor, the next half hour passed in a blur of activity.

"I've already called for plane reservations," Michael informed Laura, when she asked Kattie for permission to phone the airline. "You leave for Phoenix at twelve from Oakland Airport."

"Thank you," Laura said, putting a soft hand on Michael's arm. Then she dashed toward the bedroom she shared with Mai, but not before she threw him a smile he would treasure forever. He found himself following behind her, unable to let her out of his sight for even a second.

"Mai, come help me put your things in my bag," she called to her daughter.

"Oh, Mom, I don't think I can go with you. My throat's hurting again, so are my ears. And remember that the doctor warned about me flying?"

"Lord, why now?" Laura murmured, when a quick check with the thermometer revealed that Mai indeed had a significant fever.

"Laura, don't worry about Mai," Kattie broke into her worried thoughts. "She'll be just fine with us. I'll continue giving her medication, and take her to see Dr. Green tomorrow. Together, we'll be able to handle anything."

"Honey, I'm sorry, but I guess you're right, you'll have to stay here." Laura knelt down to talk to her daughter. "Mai, I'll be truthful with you. I don't think Grandpa is going to make it this time. But I know he'll understand why you didn't come."

"Deep down?" Mai asked. "Down where he's been living all these years?"

"Yes, sweetheart," Laura agreed. "In his heart and in his soul, where he's still the grandfather you remember. He'll understand that you're sick and couldn't say good-bye."

"I'll say good-bye here," Mai said. "He'll be able to hear me just as well. But will you be all right?"

The sudden frown on her forehead reminded Michael of the fears Mai had about her mother's business trips.

"Your mom will be fine, Mai. I'll drive her to the airport and make sure she gets on the right plane."

"You'll check it out and not let her go unless it's a good one, won't you, Miguel?"

Michael just nodded and pulled Mai into his arms. "I'll make sure she comes back to you safely, honey." He whispered something in her ear and when he released the girl, she had a broad grin on her face.

Laura looked between her daughter and Mi–Miguel. She was bemused about her daughter's use of that name. When had Mai begun calling him that, Laura wondered . . . and why?

But she didn't have much more time to worry. Only allowing her a swift hug and kiss for Mai, Miguel rushed her out the door and into his waiting car.

He didn't even stop when a teenaged boy stepped out of a station wagon at the end of the driveway, his hands full of tackle and fish.

"Hi, Jeff. Your mom's home . . . and so's your dad," Michael called out the window as he slowly backed into the road. "There's also a girl inside that I think you'll want to meet. Her name is Mai. Ask her to play you a tune on her violin."

The trip to the Oakland Airport had to be the longest hour in Laura's life. She dreaded the thought that her father would die before she got to him. But realistically, even if he were still alive, she knew that he would be unaware she was there. Except, maybe, "deep down", as she had assured her daughter.

They pulled into the short-term lot, and Michael opened the trunk to get her suitcase. Laura didn't notice the second piece of luggage and the briefcase he was carrying until he placed the two pieces on the scale next to the check-in counter.

"Miguel, what's going on?" she asked, when the clerk handed him two tickets and boarding passes.

"We are," he told her, as they hurried toward the loading gates.

"What do you mean, *we*?"

"It seems that some important business just came up in Phoenix and I'll be traveling with you," he replied, pointing to the briefcase that he had placed on the X-ray conveyor belt.

Laura put her purse right behind it and moved through the people part of the metal-detection device.

Picking up their belongings, Michael handed Laura her purse and then guided her to the proper gate.

"Names," the ticket agent asked.

"Laura Easten and Michael O'Brian, the ticket for Mai Easten has been cancelled."

"That's seats 15A and B," the young man informed them.

Feeling dazed, Laura just walked beside Miguel down the accordion-walled connecting tunnel toward the airplane's hatch. She watched him charm the senior attendant at the door, who personally assisted them in locating their seats.

Miguel indicated that Laura should take the window assignment. She numbly sat down and tightened her seatbelt, while he stowed his briefcase in the compartment above.

The plane took off right on time. Laura watched the ground disappear, very aware that Miguel had taken her hand and that she had not pulled away from his warm, calloused grasp. She acknowledged to herself that she needed his support at that moment, and that she was very grateful he was by her side.

She didn't believe for one moment that he had any sudden business commitment in Phoenix, but Laura didn't have the strength to question his motives for being here. She just accepted his kindness and his strength.

After they reached cruising altitude and the cabin attendant delivered the hot coffee he requested for them, Michael decided that it was time to put pride aside and play his last trump card.

Putting his barely touched cup on Laura's tray, he closed his own and stood up to retrieve his briefcase. Sitting down again, he slowly opened it up and looked inside at the small stack of envelopes. Michael was aware that Laura was giving the briefcase quick sidelong glances.

When he looked at her, she reddened slightly. "Your last-minute business?" she queried.

"No, this business is more than fifteen years old, and it's about time I tied it up," he said.

Confused at the wealth of emotion in those enigmatic words, it took Laura several seconds to realize that Miguel was holding something out to her. And when she finally looked at what he had in his hand, she saw a half dozen or so envelopes—the kind made of ultra-light paper and stamped *Correo Aereo*. They were just the sort of airmail stationery she had used in Ecuador.

Her head snapped up and her eyes were captured by the powerful purpose radiated from Miguel's green irises.

"Just read them," he said softly. "I know what kind of strain you're under now, but I want you to read these before you have to deal with your father's illness. We'll talk about them later."

Compelled by the warmth in his voice, Laura opened the top envelope and read the first page. It was a letter dated fifteen years earlier, in her own handwriting.

"Miguel,

Given how we parted last week, it's probably stupid of me to write to you. But when I heard about Antisana's eruption, and that you and several other Volunteers had gone into the Oriente to help with the rescue and cleanup operations, I couldn't help but be worried about all of you.

The people of San Gabriel are getting together supplies to aid their stricken countrymen. Perhaps you could send a list of what is most needed, so that we don't duplicate the effort of others.

Keep safe, and know that many prayers go with all of you.

Laura.

Laura's hands were shaking badly by the time she opened the next letter. It was faded and blotched by mildew stains. But when she held it to the light coming through the window, she was able to make most of it out. It was dated the day of the eruption and was slightly incoherent.

"Dearest Laura,

I don't know if you'll ever forgive me, but I want you to know how much I love you. I've got to be the biggest coward in the world for running off like I did yesterday. But seeing you with your father, and realizing he was *that* Nordheim, was just too much for me to handle.

Can you understand what it was like for me? To have heaven in my grasp, and then have it all snatched away? All I could think of was that there was nothing I could give you that you didn't already have. I didn't know how I could ever provide you with the kind of life you were used to.

Those words kept going through my head, as I literally ran through the streets. Even this morning, I don't remember much about the next hour or so. But when I finally came to my senses, I was on an express bus, bound for Otovalo . . .''

The rest of the letter told the same story Miguel had related to Laura in the Corporate Lounge of the Sir Francis Drake Hotel. As she read through the other letters in the small stack, Laura found that Miguel had alternated hers with his.

The words had been written over a decade and a half before, but Laura vividly remembered the increasing desperation she had felt. And Miguel's letters mirrored the same heightening feeling of doom: the doom of their love for each other.

Tears were streaming down her face when she read the last of her letters, and failed to find the one that contained her address. Laura no longer doubted that it had been purposely destroyed.

She looked up at Miguel, helpless to say what was in her heart. But, as he had promised, he didn't press her for any commitment now that she knew he had been telling the absolute truth about their thwarted love affair. Instead, he just squeezed her hands and then gathered the letters together and placed them back in the briefcase.

For the rest of the flight his comforting arm encircling her shoulder helped strengthen her for the ordeal she faced ahead.

After landing in Phoenix, they immediately rented a car. When they pulled out of the airport, Laura guided Miguel to the Scottsdale nursing home, where her father had lived for the last five years.

It had only been a month since Laura had last seen her father, but she almost couldn't recognize the shrunken, frail man laying on the hospital bed.

Gustav Nordheim—the real Gustav Nordheim—had been gone a long time. But until now, he had always *looked* like her father. His long illness had literally been all in his head. The mental ravages of Alzheimer's disease had first imprisoned, and then destroyed the wide-ranging intellect of one of the Earth's finest minds.

That had been a great tragedy—for her father, for herself and Mai, and for the world. But at least his body had only aged as expected for a man of sixty. It had given Laura some small measure of comfort.

Today, even that illusion was gone. Even before his doctor came in to silently shake his head, Laura knew that her father would not survive the night.

She sat this last vigil at his bedside, holding his hand and talking to him in English and in German, reliving the years they had spent together when she was young. Then she told him about Mai, and how brilliant and talented his granddaughter was and what a magnificent woman she would be someday.

Michael sat in the shadows of the room, watching and listening to Laura talk far into the night. Around three in the morning her voice had become a hoarse whisper, but he did nothing to stop her. She needed to do this more than anything else right now.

He must have nodded off in his chair at one point because he awoke with a start, and realized Laura had fallen silent. She was standing by the bed, looking at her father. As he watched, Michael saw her bend down to place a kiss on her father's cheek. Laura then touched the button that summoned the nurse.

"He's gone," she said in a cracked whisper when the woman appeared. Laura gazed down at the still figure that once had housed her father's giant intellect, and she watched while the nurse verified what she already knew.

The woman turned and said sympathetically to Laura, "Why don't you go home to rest for a while. You can come back at eight, and speak with the nursing supervisor about how you want to handle the details."

"Go home?" Laura said in confusion.

But Miguel was already at her side. "I've rented a room for you nearby," he said, putting an arm around her shoulder. He led her out of the nursing home and into the car. Laura remembered little of the trip, or even entering the motel room. She was only vaguely aware that Miguel removed her shoes and dress and tucked her wearing only her slip into the bed.

"Where are you going?" she asked in sudden panic at the sound of the door opening.

"I'm just in the next room," Michael replied.

"Please don't go. Don't leave me," she begged.

"No, I won't leave you," he said, quickly shedding his shoes and jacket. He slid under the covers and wrapped his arms around her shaking body, holding her until the trembling stopped and she slid into a sleep of exhaustion.

He wanted to stay awake to monitor her sleep, her dreams, but eventually the heat generated by the soft little furnace in his arms relaxed his muscles and led him to join her in a healing slumber.

FIFTEEN

"Laura, *querida*, we have to get up. Laura, are you all right?"

The concern in Miguel's voice finally made Laura open her eyes. She knew that she had to go back to the nursing home. But for the last half hour, she had been skipping in and out of sleep, finding it almost impossible to give up the warm, safe haven of his arms.

"Miguel, you didn't leave me," she whispered sleepily, slipping away for a few seconds once more.

The surprised relief Laura had expressed made Michael wince inwardly. It tore at his heart that he had been among the people she loved, who had abandoned her in one way or another.

"I promise that I'll never leave you, Laura," he vowed, pulling her closer. "I'm not going to chicken out again. And I swear, I won't die on you—not until I'm a hundred and two."

His cheek rubbed over her shoulder, affectionate, yet undemanding. Yet, the simple gesture caused Laura's toes to curl, as galloping hormones finally woke her up and gave marching orders to every part of her body.

Sometime in the night, Miguel had undone the waistband of his slacks and unbuttoned his shirt. Unerringly, Laura's hands found the naked skin of his chest. Her fingers glided over the smooth, wide expanse and traced delicate circles around tight male nipples.

Michael groaned, grabbing her hands. "Laura, please stop. We can't, not now."

"I need to, Miguel. I want to touch your warm skin, to feel your arms tighten around me. I need your body to drive out the fear I can barely control."

Then Michael understood. After a night-long vigil with death, Laura wanted an affirmation of life. She needed to reassure herself that she still existed, that *he* and their love were alive in a universe that had mostly brought her loss and separation.

Quickly shedding his clothing, he then took longer to caress hers away. "Now, *querida*, come to me," he said when they were both naked. "Come to me, and let me prove how much I love you."

Michael lay back against the pillows and watched while Laura inspected his body with intense concentration. She seemed to be tracking the very surge of his blood, as her light touches and gentle explorations caused the quickening of that most male part of him.

She crooned words of love and praise, as her mouth and tongue teased—tasting, probing, wetting—until Michael could stand no more.

He reached for Laura and pulled her down next to him. Lifting her leg over his hips, he clasped her round bottom firmly and began to move, to stroke long, hard rhythms against the outer satin of her moist center. And when neither of them could wait a second longer, he plunged into the hot, tight place awaiting him.

In that instant, Laura's lips captured his and her tongue delved into his mouth—seeking, questing, desperate to find any dark secret he might have hidden from her.

But there were no longer any secrets keeping them apart. They gave everything to each other, denying nothing. And in the moment when a shuddering riptide of pleasure tore through their bodies, their fused lips caught each other's exaltant cry.

Awake and asleep, Michael was by Laura's side for the next two days, helping her sort out all the details concerning her father's death. He held her hand when she called to tell Mai of her grandfather's passing. He stood by her while she signed the legal papers the nursing home and the state of Arizona required. He supported her trembling body as the funeral director gave her an urn containing her father's ashes.

And later that same day, after she received a call from her father's lawyer, Michael sat by her side while the simple will was read.

"That's the legal terminology, Mrs. Easten. The upshot is that your father's estate provided for his maintenance as long as he lived, but there is nothing left over for you or your daughter. On the other hand, there are no bills outstanding to trouble you, either."

Laura managed a bleak smile, nodding her head to acknowledge that she knew what it was like to have to pay a loved one's remaining debts. It would take a few more years for her to settle Jerry's medical bills.

"Mr. Harrison, thank you for all you have done on behalf of my father over these last several years." Laura said, gathering her purse up to leave.

"Before you go, there is one final matter. This is for you," the lawyer said, picking up a sealed letter from a file folder and handing it to her.

"From my father," she told Miguel, after seeing her name written in Gustav Nordheim's distinctive handwriting on the envelope. She tucked it into her purse to read in the privacy of their motel room.

After saying good-bye to the lawyer, Miguel took Laura's arm and guided her to the rental car. On the short ride back to the motel, her mood darkened. And by the time they reached the room, Laura was actually shaking.

Somehow, she knew the thin letter in her purse held painful information, information that would only add to her grief.

After opening the door for her, Miguel gave Laura a warm kiss on the cheek, telling her to get some rest before dinner.

"I'll just go down to the manager's office and settle our bill. And I'll also call the airline to schedule our return trip for early tomorrow morning."

"Oh, good. That sounds fine," she said distractedly, as she stood staring at the handbag she had put on the dresser. After a few seconds, Laura realized that Miguel was trying to give her some privacy to read her father's farewell and she loved him for his perception and tact.

She lifted her head to tell him so, but the door had already closed behind him. Sighing, Laura went to change into a robe. Then she brushed her teeth and her hair. About to search her purse for an emery board to file her nails, she shook her head in disgust at her cowardice and pulled out the letter instead.

Sitting in an easy chair, she turned on the nearby table lamp and opened the envelope. Even in the bright light, Laura could barely read the shaky, imprecise handwriting that wandered between English and German. But finally, she made out her father's words.

It seemed that he had written her an apology. An apology in which Gustav Nordheim listed his failings as a father. Among them, he cited the frequent separations his work had caused when she was young. He also mentioned his failure to listen to her problems when he was preoccupied with the state of the world and trying to figure out how to keep the nuclear nations from blowing everyone off the face of the Earth.

Laura shook her head. Her father hadn't known that even as a teen she understood that his efforts to bring about global peace far outweighed his occasional lapses of parental attention.

Not that she hadn't put her own problems ahead of the world's a time or two. Laura smiled when one particular memory surfaced. She had burst into her father's study, sobbing. He immediately put down the phone he had been using to take her in his arms and console her, when he heard the boy she had been crazy about had asked someone else to the junior prom.

It was only later that Laura learned her father had hung up on the Secretary General of the United Nations.

Still laughing softly, Laura turned her attention back to her father's letter. When she continued reading, her smile faded, and then died. In the next paragraphs, Gustav Nordheim explained to his daughter the deception he had orchestrated in her final weeks as a Peace Corps Volunteer.

He begged Laura to understand that he had just found out the reason for his increasing forgetfulness, when he visited her that day in Quito. He had seen her rush into the building, hand in hand with Miguel, and realized that she was in love with the tall, dark, green-eyed young man.

Could he take a chance that this stranger would be able to provide for Laura, after Gustav became incapacitated? He could not. So her father had manipulated the situation, trying to make sure that Laura would eventually marry the one man he knew he could trust with her happiness— Jerrold Easten.

Without really saying it, he hinted that he had used his influence with the Peace Corps country director in Ecuador to keep her and Miguel separated as long as possible.

Waves of rage alternated with rushes of compassion, while Laura thought about her father's dilemma. But when she finally read the last part of the letter, all her anger dissolved into tears, as she learned of her father's deepest regret.

"*Aber, liebling*, the greatest sin I did to you, and to myself, was to deny the rich heritage of my parent's faith. When my family was killed by the Nazis *because* of their faith, I rebelled. I refused to follow the laws of my people anymore, and I denied God because I thought *He* had caused their deaths.

"I now know that it was not God—not their creed—that destroyed all of my family and friends. Rather, it was men without faith, without any goodness in their souls, who had done that.

"So, my last request is for you to find your roots. Discover the source of strength that I denied to you. Learn and teach all the holy days and festivals to my precious granddaughter, so that Mai knows the beauty from which she came."

When Michael entered the room a few minutes later, he found Laura sobbing, as if she had lost her father all over again. He rushed to her side and heard the crackle of paper under his foot. Scooping up the stationery that had fallen from her fingers, he placed the letter from Gustav Nordheim on the table beside her chair. But Laura pushed the pages to him.

"Read it," she managed, before again burying her head in her hands.

He couldn't make sense out of all of it, but Michael understood enough of what her father had written.

He couldn't help the flood of anger that surged through him while he read how the man had manipulated their lives. But when he continued reading, he finally saw how remorseful Gustav Nordheim had felt. Michael understood the man's reasons for pushing Laura into a marriage with someone he knew and trusted.

The last part of the letter filled him with anguish because Michael also was a man who had denied his heritage. He knew what it was like to be ashamed and angry that the very traits that made his people unique were causing them so much pain and suffering.

Gently pulling Laura's hands away from her face, he

mopped her tears away with his handkerchief and then took her in his arms.

"*Querida*, he soothed, "don't be sad. Your father only wanted what he thought was best for you. What he did was wrong, but we still have years and years to be together. Come on, honey, go wash your face and get dressed for dinner. We'll make an early night of it. I made reservations for us to go back home the first thing in the morning. There's even a stopover in Las Vegas for a few hours, and we can be married there."

"Oh, Miguel. I want to marry you tomorrow more than life. But I can't."

"Can't! Laura, God in heaven, what are you saying?"

"Didn't you read my father's letter?"

"Of course, I did. You saw me read it."

"But didn't you understand what he said?"

"Yes, he apologized for trying to run your life."

"I mean the last part, about wanting me to find my roots, to learn about my heritage. I just realized that you'll have to do the same thing before I can marry you."

"You want me to convert?" Michael all but shouted.

"No, I want you to go home, to your first home in the Taos Pueblo and find *your* roots, your heritage."

"Oh, Laura. You don't know what you're asking of me. There's nothing there for me, nothing."

"Then there's nothing here for you, either," Laura said, although it was the hardest thing she had ever done, the biggest risk she had ever taken.

She watched anger and anguish turn Miguel's hard features to living stone. The lines etching his lean cheeks deepened into fissures. The copper-colored skin, stretched over his harsh bones, heated to a hectic red.

He pushed away from her, pacing the room in four long strides, over and over again, while Laura waited for him to decide her fate.

Finally, he went to the phone and wrenched the receiver

off the hook. "Give me the airport," he snarled into the instrument.

Laura listened as he quickly, efficiently changed their reservations, and got them seats on the morning flight to New Mexico.

SIXTEEN

The pilot of the chartered plane guided the aircraft into the Taos Municipal Airport, after giving his passengers a close-up view of the Rio Grande Gorge and the spectacular bridge that spanned the six-hundred-foot chasm.

He was probably disappointed that his passengers didn't gasp and marvel at the sight. But even if he was, his professional manner never wavered. Upon executing a perfect landing, he escorted the granite-faced man and his beautiful but distracted companion out of the plane, and went to find the passengers for the return charter.

Once inside the airport building, Laura stood silently by Miguel's side as he arranged for yet another rental car. They had landed in Albuquerque early in the morning, and Miguel decided to fly directly into Taos. When Laura questioned the cost of hiring a plane, Miguel had muttered he wanted to be in and out of the Pueblo as quickly as possible, so he would pay for the convenience.

Now, after the stressful flight, Laura's nerves were stretched to a fine point. The plane had been even smaller than the ancient DC-3's she had experienced in Ecuador. And although the pilot was obviously competent, the ride from Albuquerque had been very bumpy.

To make everything worse, Miguel had barely looked at her since getting up this morning. And Laura began to fear she had made a terrible mistake in provoking this confrontation with his past.

Her state of mind wasn't helped by the fact that Miguel had refused to let her sleep last night. His lovemaking had been fierce, edged with a desperation that surpassed the needs Laura had felt the morning after her father died. But she didn't deny Miguel, not when he seemed to believe that it was going to be their last night together.

While they stood waiting for the rental agent to deliver their car, Michael watched Laura delicately hide a huge yawn behind her hand. He stifled the reflexive need to do the same thing. Like Laura, he was dead on his feet, but adrenaline poured into his system every time he thought of facing the Pueblo and his family again.

Once they got into the car, he had to fight not to grip the steering wheel so hard that his knuckles gleamed whitely through his dark skin. Stopping at the intersection with Highway 64, he took a few seconds to wipe the perspiration off his hands before turning eastward onto the road.

"Is it far to the reservation?" Laura asked, trying to cut through the tension in the car.

"No, in fact, we're already there. This is Pueblo land we're driving through," he said, gesturing to the gray-green sagebrush flats stretching away on either side of them.

Laura looked startled, and then peered around at the passing landscape. "Oh, how lovely this all is," she murmured, pointing at the aspen and pine-covered mountains to the north.

"That's the Sangre de Cristo range, the southernmost spur of the Rockies," Michael informed her. "Taos Peak is closest to us. And you're right, I think this has to be one of the most magnificent spots on earth." *As long as I don't have to live here,* he didn't say out loud.

They rode in silence for the next few minutes, until

Michael spotted the cut-off he wanted and made a left turn onto the access road leading to the Pueblo Village.

Encountering a long line of tourist vehicles, Michael slowed to a crawl. But he finally guided the car through the narrow passage between the walls of the San Geronimo Church on their right and the small adobe gatehouse where fees were taken to enter the plaza beyond.

Juan Garcia, the guard collecting fees today, didn't recognize Michael, although they had played together as children. Best friends, until Michael had refused initiation into the *kiva*, the young Garcia had joined the other kids in taunting and teasing the defiant boy Michael had been.

Celia Ochoa had married Juan's older brother a few months after Michael left for Ecuador. It was a happy marriage, blessed with four healthy children, Michael's mother had reminded him . . . over and over. Glancing at Laura, Michael wondered if he would ever hold a child of his own—Laura's child. Not likely, if he couldn't pass this crazy test she had set for him.

When Juan leaned down to look in the car and asked if they had any photographic equipment, Michael just said no, not telling the man that he wasn't a tourist and that he had been registered on tribal rolls at birth.

Yet, Michael realized that even if he wasn't a sightseer, he *was* just a visitor today and he handed over the money.

After pulling into a parking space near the river that bisected the Pueblo, Michael got out to look at the place he had called home the first decade and a half of his life. It hadn't seemed to change much since he had last been here, five years ago for Sara's wedding.

The two multi-storied buildings still faced each other across the Taos River, glowing gold in the afternoon sun. His exceptional memory told him that the ladders and drying racks were still in the very same locations they had always been.

Taking Laura's arm, he led her through the stream of tourists going into and out of the plaza.

"There are so many people," Laura said, sidestepping a woman who was carrying three large pots in her arms.

"Oh, about half-a-million tourists pop in and out of here every year. It's like living in a stone-aged fishbowl," Michael informed her, bitterly.

Laura looked around her. So many people and yet, the Pueblo was almost spotlessly clean. The hard-packed ground was dusty, but looked as if it had been swept that very morning.

And all around her rose ancient, golden adobe walls, broken only by the squares and rectangles of turquoise-painted window and door frames. Miguel led her around a large, domed structure. And Laura remembered seeing the same beehive pueblo ovens near Albuquerque when she and Mai stopped for some sightseeing on their move out to California three years ago.

The thick-walled structures baked the bread that the inhabitants of the Pueblo used at home and sold to tourists.

She stopped to inhale the wonderful aroma coming out of the nearest oven. Laura wanted to wait and see the finished product, but at Miguel's insistent tug on her arm, she allowed herself to be guided around a corner.

There was another, bigger oven next to the building. And one of those skinny ladders propped against the adobe wall. It was to the ladder that Miguel headed.

"You're not going up t–there, are you?" Laura stuttered, when he placed his hand on the rung just above his head.

"Of course, I am. How am I going to 'find my roots?' " he asked with more than a trace of acid in his voice. "I was born right up there, in a second-level apartment. Come on, Laura, let's go rediscover my heritage."

"But I can't go up there, not on that . . . that flimsy thing. Isn't there any other way?"

"Perhaps you'd like to take an elevator? Sorry to tell you, sweetheart, but I'm afraid there isn't one. No electricity, no elevator."

"But I can't. I've never been able to climb ladders,"
Laura said, trying to make Miguel understand. "And this
one looks like it's a hundred years old."

"It very well may be. But it's safe, Laura. Come on,
Easten, I'm not going to confront my past without you.
I've accepted your challenge, but according to you we
can't get married unless I go up there. So, it seems that
our future is in your hands."

Laura felt a twanging jolt of déjà vu. She suddenly
remembered a dusty track at the University of Maryland,
and Miguel looking down at her with just the same mixture
of humor and disappointment in his green eyes.

And like she had during Peace Corps training, Laura
knew that she would do anything to earn his admiration.
Walking up to the ladder, she swung the strap of her purse
securely over her shoulder before grabbing onto the side
rails with both hands.

"Now, you come up right behind me," Laura demanded, putting one foot on the first rung and then lifting
herself to the second.

"My pleasure," Miguel murmured, standing close to
her, his body against hers.

She glared down at him over her shoulder when he
ascended the first step, and she felt the intimate press of
his thighs against her bottom. But the thought of some
tourist coming around the corner and seeing them almost
fused together, gave Laura the impetus to put her foot on
the next rung and enter into—what was for her—virgin
territory in ladder climbing.

That leap of faith caused her to start trembling.

"Don't worry, *querida*, I won't let you fall," Michael
encouraged, all traces of amusement gone from his voice
when he felt her panic.

With his strength to count on, the fourth step was easier
than the third. And by not looking anywhere but at the
wall slowly passing in front of her, Laura made it to the

fifth rung. Her eyes peeked over the rampart surrounding the second-level roof and she felt a rush of confidence.

But then, a large hand stroked an impudent caress on an intimate part of her body, and with a little shriek Laura used the upwardly projecting side rails of the ladder to launch herself over the last rung.

The force of that effort made her hit the surface at a run. Laura was halfway across the hard-packed dirt before she could stop herself. Directly in front of her, a pretty, dark-haired woman sat in an open doorway, sanding a large, beautifully symmetrical pot, which she held firmly on her lap.

"I'm sorry, miss, but this part of the Pueblo is off-limits to visitors," the woman said, smiling regretfully as Laura looked down at her. But then the potter's eyes slid past Laura, to the tall man who had slowly come up behind her.

"Miguel! Is that you?" she called.

"No one else," he said, taking Laura by the shoulder and leading her closer.

"Well, good. You've gotten here just in time to help me do some replastering." She carefully put down the pot she had been working on and brushed the sparkling micaceous clay dust from her jeans.

"Laura, I'd like you to meet my sister, Sara Jaramillo," Michael began, knowing that Sara would rather bite her tongue off than impolitely ask who it was he had brought with him. "Sara, this is Laura Easten, my fiancée."

He threw Laura a look that dared her to dispute that designation. But she just smiled and held her hand out to his sister. The woman hesitated a second, then wiped her fingers on her jeans and took Laura's hand.

It was a quick, strong gesture of welcome. Laura had just enough time to notice the roughness of Sara's skin and the strength in her grip.

"I'm very glad to meet you," she said, belatedly recognizing that Sara was the subject of several pictures she had seen on Miguel's walls.

"And I'm glad to meet you, Laura. Especially if you had anything to do with getting my brother back here to visit," she said, giving Miguel a knowing nod of her head.

"Sara, where is everybody else?" Michael asked, when no one came out of the family apartment at the sound of his voice.

"Oh, they're at the summer house," she explained to her brother, and then said to Laura. "That's a small farm my father inherited where we keep horses and have a fruit orchard. We'll go over later. First, there's the matter of some adobe that needs fixing."

Without another word, she went to a wheelbarrow that Laura noticed was filled with dirt and straw. Sara lifted a bucket of water and began pouring it into the mixture.

Laughing with resignation, Michael shed his jacket and picked up a thick branch, which he used to stir the mud to the proper consistancy.

An hour later, Laura looked down at her slacks, admiring the elegance of adobe-caked linen. The pants would never be the same, but she would not have missed the experience of helping Sara and Miguel apply the plaster to the low ramparts surrounding the apartment. It hadn't been as easy as Laura thought in the beginning. It seemed that there was a definite knack in getting the stuff to stay on, which she found out after her first several attempts.

But just before they were finished, she managed to do it right, earning a smile of approval from the siblings.

"Well, let's wash up and then go to the summer house," Sara said, leading them into the apartment.

Laura didn't know what to expect. But it wasn't the huge, beautiful room that they entered. The walls were a symphony of textures. Rough, whitewashed plaster served as a backdrop for dozens of matte desert landscapes and bright woven tapestries—much like Miguel's collection in California.

Her eyes roamed the room, finding that the ceiling was supported by round, exposed beams—*vigas*, as the Spanish called them, and that there was a hard-packed earthen floor.

Remembering what Miguel had said about no electricity within the ancient Pueblo buildings, Laura noticed that there were no electrical outlets in the walls. And she quickly located the oil lamps that were placed strategically around the room.

Michael watched Laura examine the apartment in which he had lived, along with his sisters and parents. Her eyes were so expressive, he could almost read her thoughts in them.

He saw that she was enchanted with the place. And as her attention moved to the adobe seating *banco* jutting out from the near wall, he watched her fall in love with the selection of prize-winning pottery the family displayed there.

Michael wondered how long it would take her to realize that the other earthen shelves were used for sleeping, and that except for the small kitchen, there wasn't another room in the apartment—no bedrooms, no dining room, no bathrooms, and not a bit of privacy.

He couldn't quite keep from chuckling when it happened, ten seconds later. Laura looked wildly around for doors that weren't there, and then lifted dazed, questioning eyes to his.

But, hey, this was a former Peace Corps Volunteer! And he saw her quickly rally before turning to speak to Sara.

"What a marvelous home you have. Absolutely unique. And these pots are the most beautiful I've ever seen."

Laura's hand hovered over one of the glowing vessels, torn by the overwhelming desire to caress its bright surface and trying to remember that she was only a guest here.

"Go ahead, pick it up," Sara said with a laugh. "They're made to be touched, to be used. Unlike some of the stuff done in other pueblos, Taos pottery holds water and you can cook in it.''

"You did all of these?" Laura asked, picking up the nearest beauty and stroking its gleaming finish.

"A lot of them. That's how I earn my living, by making little clay pots. My mother's are better, though.''

"Don't let Sara kid you, Laura. After getting degrees from the University of New Nexico, and the Institute of American Indian Art, in Santa Fe, she has shops and galleries in half a dozen states, all begging her to supply them with anything she makes.''

"Oh, go on with you and your Irish blarney, O'Brian," Sara laughed.

But Laura saw how pleased she was with Miguel's compliment. As the young woman led them into the kitchen to wash, the skin on her high cheekbones glowed with a lovely rose-brown blush.

While rinsing off her hands with river water that had been poured from a bucket, Laura noticed Miguel looking around the room, a worried frown creasing his forehead.

"Sara, where is Mother's collection of *Kachina* dolls?''

"Oh, she took them with her to the summer house."

"Why? She's never done that before.''

"She wanted them with her, now that the family's living over there permanently.''

"Permanently?"

"Yes, Miguel. You know about her arthritis. Well, it's gotten really bad lately, and she just couldn't manage going up and down the ladders anymore. You know how she'd feel if she were stuck indoors all the time. So, Dad moved them over last year.''

"Why didn't anyone write to me? I know some top-flight specialists who can help her. There're lots of things that can be done—should be done—to keep her condition from deteriorating any further.''

"Well, I agree, but you know how she is. You fight with her when we get there.''

"Sara, I don't understand. If they all moved to the summer house, why are you here? In fact, why aren't you in Santa Fe?"

"Oh, I gave up my place in Santa Fe," Sara said lightly. "I've decided to polish my white Taos boots and try living in the Pueblo, as close to the old ways as possible for a while."

Laura didn't understand exactly what Sara meant, but a shadow had crossed the young woman's face, and she sensed a thousand unsaid sorrows in that terse statement.

"What does your husband think about living here?" Miguel asked, remembering meeting Jorge Jaramillo at the wedding and talking to the smart, ambitious young man Sara had married.

"Jorge's opinion doesn't matter. I filed for a divorce last month."

"Sara!"

"Look, Miguel. Let's not discuss this. Just let me tell you that Jorge got a job offer to head a computer department in San Jose, California, and I refused to go. My fault, not his, end of discussion. Now, Laura, let me take you to our farm, so you can meet my parents."

Michael forded the stream that edged the Montoya property in one long leap. He reached back to give his hand to Laura, helping her jump across. Once they rounded a stand of twisted old apple trees, the single-storied adobe ranch house came into view in the distance.

It sat under the shade of an ancient cottonwood. Michael had always loved this place. And wished that he could have lived here all year long, and not just during summer vacations.

He often thought he might not have left the Pueblo at all, if he could have stayed in this house. There were horses to ride when he needed to feel free of thick, confining walls. And there had been fields to plant and hoe, which helped burn away the restless energy that had always plagued him.

Unlike the Pueblo apartment, Will had installed electricity and sunk a well here. And to the young boy Miguel had been, that had been enough of a modern miracle to have kept him content for years.

Well, maybe not content, he thought ruefully. He would still have been an outsider, even in his own family. That's what he hoped Laura would see today, what he hoped to prove to her. She had to realize that there was nothing here for him.

Laura almost fell flat on her face, twisting and turning, trying to take in the wealth of beauty surrounding her. The mountains behind the house, the clear stream to their right, the small orchard laden with growing apples—the whole setting was absolutely awe inspiring. She didn't know how Miguel had ever left, or why he didn't want to come back to live here.

He had pulled a little ahead of her and Sara, and as they neared the low adobe house, his long legs ate up the distance, almost as if he couldn't wait to get home. He rushed around a corner, disappearing from sight.

Laura's heart lightened at his impatience. Maybe everything would be all right, and he would make peace with his past today.

"I really do thank you for making Miguel come back to visit," Sara said in a soft voice, her steps getting shorter and shorter, until she stopped to look intently at Laura. "It *was* your idea, wasn't it?"

"Yes," she admitted, "but he was so angry with me for forc–"

"For forcing him to come?" Sara finished, when Laura tried to censor what she had been about to say. "Don't worry, we all know how he feels about the Pueblo."

"But, why? It's so wonderful here. I've never seen sky so deep blue, or smelled air that was so clean. And the Pueblo . . . well, as I said before, it's unique."

"All that is true. And for years, I couldn't understand why it was not enough for Miguel, either. But I finally figured out the problem. *Miguel* is unique, and the Pueblo requires us to conform. He is brilliant, but we do not want anyone to shine brighter then the rest. We are committed to a continuation of the past, and Miguel lives with the future always in his thoughts.

"So he would never be happy living here. I think everyone in the family has accepted that. We just hope he's found what he needs in California."

Laura looked at Sara carefully, debating whether to tell her just how lonely her brother had been. Her love for Miguel won out over her fear of offending his sister.

"Sara, Miguel does have a successful business and a wonderful home in the San Francisco area, which I saw for the first time just a few days ago. But Sara, now that I've come to Taos, I see that Miguel tried to recreate in his home, everything he loved best in the Pueblo.

"The walls of his house are thick adobe, there are *vigas* supporting the ceilng, and his bedroom is a loft that he gets to by climbing a *kiva* ladder. You don't know it, but he has pictures of you and your sisters all over the place. And now that I've seen your work, I think that he's bought as many of your pots as he could find to display in his living room."

Laura waited a minute for some sort of reaction, but Sara just stood there, her dark eyes following the play of the wind through the leaves.

"Sara! He's prepared a beautiful bedroom for your younger sisters. And I wouldn't be surprised if there weren't others just waiting for you and your parents. But you all refuse to visit him. Why? Why did he have to be so alone for so long?"

Sara pressed her face against the bark of the nearest tree, and Laura saw her shoulder begin to shake. Feeling a wave of remorse for her vehement words, she was just going to apologize for being so blunt, when Sara turned to her.

She scrubbed away tears from her cheeks, but she smiled at Laura.

"I am so glad that you're going to marry Miguel, Laura. He's needed someone to love him like you do for such a long time. But let me explain something that you might not know about us . . . about the Taos. We couldn't go to Miguel. We could only wait, enduring our sadness, until something happened to bring him back home.

"Laura, I know it's strange to you, but let me give you an example of the way we live. Do you know what my ancestors did when the corn needed more water?" Sara asked rhetorically. "They didn't dig another irrigation ditch from the river. Instead, they put on their finest clothing, with bright beaded moccasins or white buckskin boots. And then they went into the plaza to dance all day for rain!"

Laura just stood there shaking her head until she finally understood what Sara was saying. And then she began to laugh. "Oh, Sara, don't tell me that Miguel will put on feathers every time I tell him to water the lawn?"

"No, I told you that he's different from the rest of us. Although I do remember a time when he stood right over there by the creek and talked to the . . ." Sara's eyes suddenly widened. "Laura . . . of course, you must be *that* Laura."

"Sara, I don't understand. What do you mean."

"Tell me, how long have you known Miguel?"

"A long time, we were both in the Peace Corps. But we . . . lost track of each other, and only met again a short while ago."

"Ah, so you are the Laura that Miguel talked about twelve years ago."

"He talked about me? To whom?"

"Oh, to the moon, to the stars, to the gods. He'd just come back from the army, and for the first and only time

I've ever seen it happen, he got drunk. Absolutely stinking. My mother was furious, and told him to go dunk his head in the stream and stay outside until he was sober.

"Well, it must have been about two in the morning when I heard him out here, talking. I snuck out and hid behind some bushes. Miguel was yelling, cursing at the *Kachinas*. He asked the gods why they let him find his Laura again, only to discover that she was married to someone else."

"Oh, Sara . . . Sara," Laura moaned, unable to bear the pain Miguel must have felt. "I waited for him. I waited over two years, but . . ."

"Well, the waiting is over now. You both endured your sadness, and now it's time for you to be happy together. Come on, Laura, come meet your in-laws-to-be."

Laughing like schoolgirls, they all but ran around to the front entrance of the Montoya ranch house.

Laura stopped short when she saw that Miguel had yet to go inside. He stood gazing at the brightly painted turquoise door, his eyes burning, as if he were facing the gate to hell.

With tears forming in her eyes, Laura ran to him. Not caring that his sister was behind her, she reached up to take his lean face in her hands and pressed her warm lips to his cold mouth.

His arms instantly went round her, holding on to her like she was the only thing anchoring him to the earth.

"I love you, Miguel. I always have and I always will," she said, the extent of her feelings making her voice shake. "I adore everything you bring me—the Spanish words you whisper in the night, the cut of your Indian cheekbones, and I even like that Irish gift of gab that gets you in trouble now and then.

"Miguel, I treasure your mixed-up heritage because it's made you the man you are—the sum of all your yesterdays."

"Ah, *querida*," he crooned softly. "I don't know why

it has taken me so long to understand that. But you're right, we should cherish our past, and be thankful for all the tomorrows we'll share.'' He took her hand and resolutely led her toward the house. ''Come on, Laura, I'm going to introduce you to my mother and my other sisters, and to my stepdad.''

He pushed open the bright door.

''*Ka*? Mother, where are you? *Mamacita*, it's your son, Miguel. I've come home.''

EPILOGUE

"There, that should keep it in place if the wind stays under hurricane force," Kattie Sinclair said, fixing the picture hat to Laura's hair with a long pin. "Outdoor weddings bring a whole 'nother set of problems, don't they?"

"Tell me about it," Laura agreed with her matron of honor, and then examined the full skirt of her long peach-colored gown. "Maybe I should have sewn lead weights into the hem of my dress. With my luck, it'll fly up over my head in the middle of the ceremony."

"No, your service is going to be just perfect. That's something that would happen to me, even if I get remarried inside the church."

"So, you've finally decided to accept J.J.'s one thousandth and one proposal?"

"Yeah, I'm going to chance it again. On paper, all his plans look good. He's found several clients in the area who want him to train their horses for the show ring. And that means he won't have to work at racetracks.

"Also, J.J's got a new psychologist here and a support group. I've met with the shrink, and he thinks that J.J's a hundred-percent committed to never gambling again."

Laura picked up her bridal bouquet from the table and then looked at her friend, unable to keep the concern she felt out of her voice. "But what do *you* think, Kattie?"

"I think it's a longshot, and that I've become the gambler in the family. But I don't want to live without him anymore, so I'm keeping my fingers crossed. We've taken up the option I had to buy the house next door. The kids all love this area, and there's enough land so that we can breed horses, eventually."

"I'm glad we'll be neighbors," Laura smiled. "It'll be such fun to . . ." At the sound of an expressive piano arpeggio, she stopped talking and clutched at Kattie's hand.

"Well, Jeff's all geared up, so I guess it's time for you to get yourself married," Kattie informed her. With a light kiss on Laura's cheek, her friend picked up her own spray of flowers and then went out to find the best man.

Taking a deep breath, Laura followed Kattie out of Miguel's house. She stopped under the shaded patio overhang, looking at the hundred friends and relatives who were standing on either side of the grassy aisle.

Marthe was front row center, next to Elena Montoya and her three daughters. And right beside Sara, stood her estranged husband, Jorge Jaramillo. The two of them were just inches apart, but still not together.

There was a subtle shift in the music, as Kattie and the best man took their places.

Laura heard a wave of appreciation ripple through the assembled guests, when Will Montoya—in the traditional ceremonial regalia of a Taos Indian—slowly marched up the aisle with Kattie, toward the white marriage canopy at the end.

The instant the couple reached the *huppah*, and the rabbi standing under the ritual tenting, Mai's violin sang out the triumphant strains of Mendelsohn's wedding march. Lovely in a long lilac dress, she looked at her mother and gave her a smiling nod.

Jeff Sinclair, sitting at the grand piano it had taken six men to move outside, joined in with Mai, and together they filled the late summer afternoon with a rhapsody of music.

On her cue, Laura stepped away from the patio into the afternoon sunshine. She walked down the grassy green path, toward the emerald-eyed man who stood waiting for her at the other end.

As she listened to the excited whispers of friends and family following her progress, Laura felt happy that she and Miguel had taken the time to organize this wedding, rather than doing the deed quickly in Las Vegas or Reno.

She had needed the weeks to close up her apartment in Los Angeles, and get Mai registered in school for the coming semester. But most of the time had been spent trying to locate a rabbi.

A rabbi who would organize a course of study for Laura and her daughter, and who would also officiate a wedding featuring a groom named O'Brian, and a best man dressed in eagle feathers and beaded moccasins.

But all the worry about planning the ceremony dissolved like a snowball thrown on this warm August day, when Laura reached the canopy and looked deeply into Miguel's eyes.

He took her hand and never let go of it while the rabbi led them through the ancient rite. It ended with them well and truly married, with a kiss and Miguel stomping on the traditional wine glass.

A small band provided music for dancing later until a sudden hush fell over the crowd. From her haven in her husband's arms, Laura looked around and found that the entire Montoya family stood alone, in the center of the guests.

Beating on a beautifully crafted rawhide drum, Will began an insistent, heart-pounding rhythm.

As he called out a low chant, his wife and daughters started moving, their graceful bodies swaying. The buckskin fringes of their beaded robes swirled in rippling waves, while their blinding-white Taos boots glided in intimate contact with Mother Earth.

"I've never seen anything so lovely," Laura whispered up to Miguel, who stood right behind her, his arms wrapped around her waist.

"Yes, it is. But I don't know how to break this to you, Mrs. O'Brian." He chuckled as his large hand opened possessively over Laura's flat stomach. "Laura . . . your in-laws over there are doing an absolutely authentic—one hundred percent guaranteed—fertility dance."

SHARE THE FUN . . .
SHARE YOUR NEW-FOUND TREASURE!!

You don't want to let your new books out of your sight? That's okay. Your friends can get their own. Order below.

No. 65 TO CATCH A LORELEI by Phyllis Houseman
Lorelei sets a trap for Daniel but gets caught in it herself.

No. 61 HOME FIELD ADVANTAGE by Janice Bartlett
Marian shows John there is more to life than just professional sports.

No. 62 FOR SERVICES RENDERED by Ann Patrick
Nick's life is in perfect order until he meets Claire!

No. 63 WHERE THERE'S A WILL by Leanne Banks
Chelsea goes toe-to-toe with her new, unhappy business partner.

No. 64 YESTERDAY'S FANTASY by Pamela Macaluso
Melissa always had a crush on Morgan. Maybe dreams do come true!

No. 66 BACK OF BEYOND by Shirley Faye
Dani and Jesse are forced to face their true feelings for each other.

No. 67 CRYSTAL CLEAR by Cay David
Max could be the end of all Crystal's dreams . . . or just the beginning!

No. 68 PROMISE OF PARADISE by Karen Lawton Barrett
Gabriel is surprised to find that Eden's beauty is not just skin deep.

No. 69 OCEAN OF DREAMS by Patricia Hagan
Is Jenny just another shipboard romance to Officer Kirk Moen?

No. 70 SUNDAY KIND OF LOVE by Lois Faye Dyer
Trace literally sweeps beautiful, ebony-haired Lily off her feet.

No. 71 ISLAND SECRETS by Darcy Rice
Chad has the power to take away Tucker's hard-earned independence.

No. 72 COMING HOME by Janis Reams Hudson
Clint always loved Lacey. Now Fate has given them another chance.

No. 73 KING'S RANSOM by Sharon Sala
Jesse was always like King's little sister. When did it all change?

No. 74 A MAN WORTH LOVING by Karen Rose Smith
Nate's middle name is 'freedom' . . . that is, until Shara comes along.

No. 75 RAINBOWS & LOVE SONGS by Catherine Sellers
Dan has more than one problem. One of them is named Kacy!

No. 76 ALWAYS ANNIE by Patty Copeland
Annie is down-to-earth and real . . . and Ted's never met anyone like her.

No. 77 FLIGHT OF THE SWAN by Lacey Dancer
Rich had decided to swear off romance for good until Christiana.

No. 78 TO LOVE A COWBOY by Laura Phillips
Dee is the dark-haired beauty that sends Nick reeling back to the past.

No. 79 SASSY LADY by Becky Barker
No matter how hard he tries, Curt can't seem to get away from Maggie.

No. 80 CRITIC'S CHOICE by Kathleen Yapp
Marlis can't do one thing right in front of her handsome houseguest.

No. 81 TUNE IN TOMORROW by Laura Michaels
Deke happily gave up life in the fast lane. Can Liz do the same?

No. 82 CALL BACK OUR YESTERDAYS by Phyllis Houseman
Michael comes to terms with his past with Laura by his side.

No. 83 ECHOES by Nancy Morse
Cathy comes home and finds love even better the second time around.

No. 84 FAIR WINDS by Helen Carras
Fate blows Eve into Vic's life and he finds he can't let her go.

Meteor Publishing Corporation
Dept. 392, P. O. Box 41820, Philadelphia, PA 19101-9828

Please send the books I've indicated below. Check or money order only—no cash, stamps or C.O.D.s (PA residents, add 6% sales tax). I am enclosing $2.95 plus 75¢ handling fee for *each* book ordered.

Total Amount Enclosed: $_____.

____ No. 65	____ No. 67	____ No. 73	____ No. 79
____ No. 61	____ No. 68	____ No. 74	____ No. 80
____ No. 62	____ No. 69	____ No. 75	____ No. 81
____ No. 63	____ No. 70	____ No. 76	____ No. 82
____ No. 64	____ No. 71	____ No. 77	____ No. 83
____ No. 66	____ No. 72	____ No. 78	____ No. 84

Please Print:
Name _____
Address _____ Apt. No. _____
City/State _____ Zip _____

Allow four to six weeks for delivery. Quantities limited.